MY DREAM DATE

RAISED BY WOLVES BOOK 4

CASEY MORALES

Edited by
CARLEY SLATTERY

WWW.AUTHORCASEYMORALES.COM

PREFACE

You're going to find this hard to believe, especially when you learn how gullible I was at twenty-two when this series began, but what you're about to read is a true story. Yes, I have changed names and places to protect the guilty, and embellished here and there, but the bones of the tale are true.

What can I say? I was a modern-day Gomer Pyle.

I was *that* preacher's kid. You know, the one who never knew he was supposed to be secretly rebellious and get away with a hidden wild side. Yeah, I missed that memo. I was the PK who was *actually* into being righteous and good—whatever that means these days.

I grew up in a kind, loving household, with three older sisters. The youngest was seven years older than me, so it was like being an only child with five parents.

Now, years later, I know that was the perfect setup for coming out later in life, but at the time, I had no clue. I was convinced I would one day have a beautiful wedding in a massive church with flowers and candles everywhere.

You're snickering. How rude.

Anyway, you get the picture. Good boy. Innocent. Completely clueless. And *definitely* straight. Did I mention that? I was straight, doggone it.

I firmly believed I'd made it through high school and college without meeting a single gay person. I was convinced, as was taught from the pulpit on Sundays, that all gays lived in California or New York. I was never clear on why those two particular states had become a haven for homosexual hedonism, but as long as I stayed away from those evil places, everything would be fine. Right?

Little did I know my best friend from fourth grade through high school was a screaming queen—and not the subtle basketball-playing gay who looked sideways at the other boys in the showers. Oh no. He was the chiffon-waving, *hey-gurl*-yelling signal fire that could be seen from space.

How was I supposed to know? Just because he was the drum major in the marching band—

And your snickering continues.

I see now that we are not going to have a serious,

adult conversation, so I may as well get on with the story.

Unlike the previous tomes in this work, life in My Dream Date deals with more serious moments, times in my life when I learned truths contained barbs as often as they held bliss. The last thing I want is to throw a wet towel on our fun adventure, but real life does that sometimes—and I really am trying to stick to what happened. I hope you laugh out loud, squirm a little, get a bit overheated, and maybe even shed a tear.

Aw, who am I kidding? I just want you to laugh, and drool over the steam. Isn't that what we're all here for anyway?

Good luck, dear reader. Enjoy the ride.

Oh crap.

I said *ride*.

1

PERKY PYTHON

I stopped speaking long enough to shove another bite of waffle in my mouth. Dwayne and Jason ate quietly, attentively, allowing me to, well, waffle on without interruption. Though how Jason's ever-present shit-eating grin survived each forkful of whatever hash he was devouring, I'll never know.

"I never thought I'd fall for a guy who raises tigers and cougars for a living. In fact, now that I think about it, I never expected to fall for a guy at all." I dabbed the napkin to the corner of my mouth. "My whole world had been mapped out, complete with a fancy wedding in a packed church with my mom wailing from the front row. I guess the whole gay thing shattered that dream."

"Wait. Are you saying your mom doesn't still

want a wedding? I figured she'd bake a cake with a giant dil—"

"Jason, *behave*," Dwayne said, his voice indignant but his expression amused. "Let the boy talk. Can't you see he's excited?" He motioned with his fork for me to continue.

Jason made a childish face, and the two of them giggled. I cleared my throat to regain the floor.

"Are you two listening?" I tried to sound irritated, but it just came out squeaky. I was too giddy to be upset. "For the first time in a while, I'm *really* happy. I mean, I was happy with Carter and the kids, but I don't think I really knew what dating or a relationship *was* with him."

Dwayne snorted. "Dating? You moved in after *one* dinner. That was downright lesbionic of you."

"Lesbionic?" My brow quirked, and Dwayne smirked. "Never mind. I'm not letting either of you get me sidetracked today. I'm too excited."

"Lord. Is he pregnant? Am I going to be an uncle? What would that make you, a great-great—" Jason earned a playful slap on the arm from Dwayne.

"No, nobody's pregnant. But since you brought it up, have I told you how big—"

"YES!" Dwayne said, waving his fork, not realizing there was half a sausage stuck to it. Jason and I burst into laughter that grew louder when the offending sausage flew into the window. He tossed the fork down. "We get it. He's huge. Practically a python. Move on."

"Somebody's *sensitive* today," I quipped.

"When he doesn't get his morning Geritol, this happens," Jason added.

"I'm only forty-four!" Dwayne said.

I nodded conspiratorially at Jason, as if he'd just made our point for us, then continued. "Donny and I have been dating for a little over four months now, and it's been great. He's funny and sweet, but in a strong, real-man way. I love getting to play with the cougars. They're crazy, always sneaking and attacking. It's incredible how they coordinate. I never knew cats were that smart."

"Why do I sense a *but* coming?" Jason asked.

"But…well…I still haven't seen him naked, much less done anything with his…python."

"Wait," Jason said. "*Four* months? How do you know he's huge then?"

"We make out on the couch or in bed. Trust me, it's easy to feel through his underwear. That thing is—"

"Huge. Yes, yes. We know. Back to the lack of sex, please," Dwayne said.

I chuckled. It was fun to poke at Dwayne. He was the best friend I'd ever had. Come to think of it, he might've been one of the best people I'd ever met. He'd seen me through so much, and never asked for anything in return—other than an occasional shoulder to cry on when one of his twentysomething infatuations moved on to someone closer to their own generation.

Dwayne grounded me, but in a way that made me want to do better, to *be* better. Do all best friends do that? Or is that unique to best friends who are double your age?

Don't tell him I said that. He'll slap you. And me.

"I don't know what to think. There's no doubt he likes me—and when we make out, there's no question he's attracted. His perky python makes that clear enough. So why aren't we having sex? Is that weird? Am I thinking too much?"

Jason snorted again. "You're *always* thinking too much—unless you're doing stupid things because you're not thinking enough."

"You're one to talk about stupid, Mr. Rocket Scientist," Dwayne snarked, then turned back to me. "Have you asked him about it?"

I hesitated. "Well, not really. I mean…we talked a while back about him wanting to wait—"

"But you haven't talked about your concerns recently?" Dwayne asked.

"They're not really *concerns*," I said, a little too

defensively. "I mean, I guess they are. I'm okay waiting for sex, but I'd like to know why. It seems very un-gay of him."

Dwayne actually spit coffee across the table. It took a couple minutes for him to stop laughing long enough to speak. "You were the most un-gay gay I'd ever met, young man. You have *no* room to talk there."

"I don't know," Jason said thoughtfully. His sudden seriousness caught my attention. "Maybe Michael has a point. Most guys get naked right out of the gate, or at least early on. They want to see if the magic is there, or if Tab A really does fit into Slot B. Not getting naked after four months is pretty weird."

Silence hovered over our table until our ever-vigilant waitress, Katie, arrived.

"You three are never quiet. My alarm bells are ringing." She turned to me with both fists planted on her ample hips. "What did you do?"

"Me? Why me?"

Dwayne and Jason laughed and avoided Katie's roaming gaze.

"Because silence at this table always revolves around something you've done or someone you're dating. Don't you read the menu?"

"The menu—" Dwayne spat through hoots. "That's the best line of the day, Katie. You win."

"Oh, shut it, *old man*," I said, turning back to her. "We're just talking about a guy."

"Shocked face," she said, scooting into the booth beside me. "Out with it. Aunt Katie is here now. Ignore whatever stupidity those two told you."

"Hey!" Dwayne feigned offense. She raised a brow and he settled back into his seat, unwilling to duel with a superior opponent.

Katie listened attentively as I recounted our conversation, sans the part about the perky python.

"Honey, you need to talk to him. Just ask him why waiting is important to him. If he really cares about you, he'll appreciate the open dialogue."

"That's what I told him," Dwayne huffed from behind his coffee mug.

"Zip it." Katie made a zipper signal with her fingers across her lips. "Michael, if you can't talk openly about everything, he's not good enough for you. Trust me. I've dealt with my share of closed-off men. They're not worth it."

There was such sincerity in her eyes. I thought there might've been a little pain in there too. As long as we'd been coming to the diner, as many times as Katie had been part of our conversations, I realized we really didn't know *her* story at all. I'd have to fix that. Later, after I'd dealt with Mr. No Sex.

"Thanks, Katie. You're the best," I said as we hugged.

"Oh, I know. Make Dwayne add a counseling fee to today's tip." She winked, grabbed our empty plates, and hustled away.

2

THE BIG GAY BUBBLE

Donny had left for a zookeeper conference in San Diego and wouldn't return until the weekend. Thanks to the bar's revolving door of employees, he was one of two bartenders available to work, so our next date was on the books for Sunday night. That gave me plenty of time to obsess—I mean, *think carefully*— about the conversation I wanted to have.

Ironically, during that same week, I finally flew the proverbial nest. After working with my dad since graduating from college, I left the family business and started a new job in the real world. It was exciting and frightening, and all the things people normally feel when they start their first big-boy job, only I was doing it at twenty-seven years old.

Let's just call the time with my dad my master's

degree in running a small business and move on, shall we?

On Monday morning, I donned my cleanest, least-wrinkled khakis and a light blue polo shirt, grabbed a tumbler full of coffee from the kitchen, and drove to my new office. The company was relatively young—and small. There were only a few senior people, and a dozen worker bees like me. It felt a lot like a family business.

Apparently, the gods of employment had a sense of humor.

We sold IT equipment and computer services to companies. There were teams of salespeople, computer engineers, and software programmers, along with a few muckety-mucks who mostly drank coffee and smoked cigars out back. I later learned the muck-eties were related, completing the employment gods' circle of irony.

The sales guys (and one gal) were exactly what you'd expect: type A go-getters who thrived on the hunt. There was so much testosterone in that group, even with the lone female, that their corner of our office practically vibrated with energy.

Separated by a thin barrier of scrunchy room-divider stuff—no, I don't know what that's called— were the engineers. Imagine if *Star Trek* and *Star*

Wars had a baby. That's an IT engineer. The level of nerdiness on their side of the Great Wall far outpaced the testosterone on ours. They were nice enough folks, and super smart, but I half expected a game of Dungeons and Dragons to break out at any moment.

Then there were the programmers. We only had five of those critters, and they kept to themselves in a separate room. I guess it made sense to segregate them. They needed to concentrate, or one *01* might turn into a *10* and there goes the program.

But what did I know? I was a sales guy. We were tasked with finding companies who needed computers, or computer help, or a computer upgrade, or anything to do with computers. We were bred to be stupid and promise the world, regardless of what the engineers and programmers claimed was possible— and we drove those poor people crazy.

In truth, we did push the envelope, but much to their chagrin, the engineers usually found a way to make our promises a reality for clients. They might've used duct tape and paperclips, but they made shit happen.

All hail the pocket protector!

A few hours into my first day, the owner asked me to join him in his office. Gary was a rail-thin man with bottle-bottom glasses that made his eyes appear bugged out. His massive front teeth rarely allowed him to close his lips, so two Bugs Bunny teeth were usually visible, resting happily on his bottom lip. It looked like he had tried to grow a beard, but, like many nerds of the programming clan, it wasn't genetically possible. Scraggly patches of brown and graying hair looked more like a swamp on a map than a beard. He was a nice dude, but man was he a candidate for one of those makeover shows. Unfortunately for him, the original Fab Five were still a few years away from zhuzhing their way around America's most clueless straight guys.

As we entered his office, my boss, Rick, who was standing by Gary's desk, waved me in. The contrast between the two company leaders couldn't have been starker. Rick stood at six three, weighed a solid two-eighty, and had once been a strapping college football player. Now, his belly was wider than his broad shoulders, but the football-player frame was still visible. Rick was an outdoor-lovin', pickup-drivin', boot-wearin' slab o' man—and he oozed 'sales guy.'

With two enormous strides, he crossed the room and gripped my hand with a vice-like paw, while his other hand squeezed my arm. "Good to see you again, Michael. We're really happy you joined our team."

Gary shuffled around his desk and sat, adjusted his

bottle-bottoms, straightened the four pens I hadn't noticed on his desk, then blinked up at me. "Right," he said. "We want to give you a welcome gift. Rick?"

Rick reached behind the desk and pulled out a shiny white jacket with *Crystalogic* scrawled in thumb-sized script across the left chest. Each letter of the company's name was shaded a different color, creating a rainbow out of the logo.

My mouth dropped open at the *obvious* gay reference.

"You like it?" Rick asked as he handed me the coat.

"Yeah, it's nice. Thanks, guys."

"Gary named the company, but I came up with the logo myself," Rick said. "Saw a bumper sticker on a car in front of me at the McDonald's drive-through that read 'Family Values' in rainbow colors, thought it sent a nice message about what we stand for."

I looked to Gary. His bland expression didn't waver. "We're a family company. We do what's right for the customer above our own interest. We treat each other right. Stuff like that."

Sweet baby Jesus, they didn't know what the bumper sticker *really* meant—and they had crafted the company's image around something they thought was more about church than, well, families with two daddies or mommies.

Like a good little rookie employee, I donned my jacket while swallowing hard to keep from laughing. When I looked up, both men were smiling.

Who was I to burst their big gay bubble?

3

AN UNEXPECTED DINNER GUEST

Friday night was a high school basketball night, and I refereed eight back-to-back AAU games on Saturday. By the time I got home Saturday evening, my legs were wobbly. The thought of visiting Donny at the bar popped into my head, but my body revolted. I ate Cheerios for dinner, watched a rerun of some '80s comedy, then passed out.

On Sunday evening, I knocked politely on Donny's door, then let myself in. The sumptuous smell of bacon frying made my stomach do somersaults.

"I'm in the kitchen. Go say hi to the kids while I finish dinner."

The *kids* Donny referred to were three cougar cubs he was hand-raising before their life at Nashville Zoo began. When I first met the little terrors, they were barely larger than a newborn infant. Now, they'd dwarf a mid-sized dog. It had been fun to watch them grow, but also sad. They were clearly outgrowing the confines of a crate and needed room to roam and hunt —and do whatever it is that frisky cougars do all day.

But for another month or so, they were our kids.

As soon as I opened the bedroom door, the playful growls and groans began. Theo pawed impatiently at the metal of the cage.

Yes, his name was Theo. The other chipmunks were Alvin and Simon. It turned out that zookeepers had an odd sense of humor that directly translated into their naming convention. Who knew?

Theo was the assassin, the incredibly intelligent, sneaky little bugger who loved to ninja his way behind me and attack my back. Alvin was the other sneak, only his attacks usually came from the side. Simon acted all sweet and innocent, lowering his head for a good scratch and purring loudly, then curling up in my lap—all as a distraction for his brothers. As soon as Theo pounced, Mr. Sweet and Cuddly's claws came out, and he'd join the assault. Those cats planned and coordinated their attacks as well as any Navy SEAL team.

And I loved every minute of it.

Except for their teeth. You know, the needle teeth every kitten has that pierces the skin no matter how light or hard they bite? Donny had rubber tips glued to their claws to protect us from their daggers, but nothing could stop those teeth. By the time my savior arrived to announce dinnertime, my hands and arms were bleeding from several tiny puncture wounds—but they were worth it. Those cats made me laugh more than a whole building full of Crystalogic engineers.

"Should I put your dinner in a cat dish and feed you all together?" Donny said from the doorway.

Simon darted toward him and nearly escaped into the house, but Donny blocked him with an expert Jackie Chan leg sweep that stopped the furball in his tracks. I stood and began loading them back into their crate, something easier said than done when there were three of them and only one of me. You know the expression "herding cats?" Yeah, that's what it was—squirming, squealing, and nipping all the way.

"You've actually gotten pretty good at that." Donny chuckled. "Come on. I made a chicken dish from a recipe for Outback's Alice Springs Chicken I found online."

I hopped to my feet and gave him a peck on the cheek. "You had me at Alice Springs Chicken."

He laughed and dragged me into the kitchen by the front of my shirt.

As with every meal I'd enjoyed at Chez Donny,

the faux Alice Springs Chicken was fabulous. I didn't know how he did it, but it tasted exactly the same as I remembered from Outback, minus the buttery bread and Boomin' Onion. One can only expect so much from his home-cook boyfriend.

Donny told me about a new keeper the zoo had hired, a bird guy. I'd met the creepy snake handler, the elephant family, and was dating the cat guy, but I'd yet to meet a bird keeper. Each animal expert I'd met had mirrored the animals they kept with startling similarity. Donny's personality and mannerisms reminded me of the Bengal tigers and lions. Even the cougars and their playful mischievousness made me think of him.

The elephant family comprised overly large humans whose quiet natures somehow commanded respect merely by their presence. And the snake guy may as well have climbed into one of the glass enclosures and lounged on a rock. He was all creepy, slithery snake-ness.

He described Janice, the new bird lady, as a cross between one of the elephant keepers and Beeker from *The Muppet Show*. We laughed as he mimicked her long, stiff neck and upturned chin, twisting sharply from side to side. She even had a peeping, high-pitched voice.

Zoo people cracked me up.

I told him about my first week at Crystalogic. We laughed over the logo and my new jacket, and I shared some of the engineers' better customer service stories.

It was a light, fun dinner, like always.

Until I said, "Hey, can we talk about something?"

"Sure," he replied tentatively.

I looked down at my nearly licked-clean plate. "So…I've been wanting to ask you about this, but wasn't quite sure how. I'm not upset or anything."

I hesitated.

He leaned forward. "You're not usually shy. Just say it. You know you can ask me anything."

I smiled weakly. "I know. Donny, I really like you—"

He leaned back. "Uh-oh."

"No, no. It's not like that. Please." I took a deep breath and covered my face with a palm. "I'm sorry. I'm making this a bigger deal than it should be. It's just…we've been dating almost four months now, and…well…we haven't *done* anything."

I couldn't read his expression. There was a flash of a smile at my stammering, then a crease around his eyes as the question struck home. I had no idea whether he was amused or pissed. Donny was a great guy. The last thing I wanted was to blow it over something as stupid as sex, but I couldn't keep my question bottled up any longer.

I gripped my napkin as my palms began to sweat.

He sighed. "I guess it's time we had *that* talk."

That talk? I had no idea what he meant.

He rose from his seat and squatted next to me, turning my chair so we faced each other. Then he gripped my arms with both hands and looked up. This strong veteran who'd survived more than I could imagine looked like a scared little boy.

"Michael, I wanted to wait for all that because I wanted to get to know you first, for you to get to know me."

I nodded like I understood. I didn't.

"And it's been great—better than great. I'm really falling for you."

"I feel—"

"Just let me get this out." He squeezed my arms gently. "I don't date much anymore. I mean, before I met you, I didn't date much. Guys would ask. They'd give me their numbers at the bar, but I couldn't bring myself to try again."

"Donny, I'm lost. What are you talking about?"

"Michael, I'm HIV positive."

The pleading in his eyes as he said those words pierced my heart, but I had no idea how to react, what to say, what to think. Dwayne and I had talked a little about HIV and his work with the blood bank years ago, but I didn't know anyone who was positive.

Did I?

And here he sat, waiting for me to respond.

I couldn't speak.

His eyes dropped to my fidgeting fingers. "I'm sorry I didn't tell you sooner. It's just…I really like you, and I didn't want you to run away before you got to know me."

"Run away?"

He nodded slowly. "Yeah. I used to tell guys right away, practically in the same sentence with my name. I figured they deserved to know, deserved a chance to decide for themselves if they wanted to go out with someone…like me. It was the last time I talked to a lot of them. They ran as fast as they could. Some of them barely make eye contact when they come to the bar now."

There was an ache in his voice. I wanted to reach out, to hold him, to comfort him. I wanted to tell him it would all be alright, that I would never run away.

But I couldn't move.

He looked into my eyes. His were rimmed with moisture. He waited for me to do something, to say something.

I didn't.

He sucked in a breath, gave my arms one last squeeze, and stood. "I know it's a lot, and I really hope you can see *me*, not my disease, but I'll understand if you're not comfortable dating anymore."

My heart stuck in my throat.

He started to turn away, but I had the presence of mind to stand and wrap him in a tight hug, nuzzling my head beneath his chin. I felt his chest tremble as tears began to fall. This poor man. This beautiful, amazing, poor man.

He led me to the door and kissed me goodnight, then watched as I climbed into my car and drove away. He pressed a hand against the screen door and held his wave until I was gone.

4
___

THE QUILT

When I got home, I logged into AOL and searched Google for information on HIV. A hodgepodge of pages detailed symptoms and treatments—and the lack of treatments. Images of patients with concave cheeks and distended bellies spoke of early-disease medication reactions. Other pages talked of support groups and hope for a vaccine, yet none believed a cure would come anytime soon. Several were dedicated to how HIV spread and the importance of safe sex, echoing much of what Dwayne had told me years ago.

And then I opened a page discussing life expectancy. There were pages honoring the thousands —no, the hundreds of thousands—of men lost to this terrible plague. In 1993 alone, more than three hundred thousand had died in the United States. The worldwide number was unfathomable to me.

I clicked on a link titled *Quilt Project.*

The quilt stretched the heart-wrenching length of the Mall in Washington, D.C., each square lovingly sewn in memory of someone lost to the disease. There were hearts and smiles, pictures of men and women in suits and dresses, others in sports uniforms, still more playing instruments or singing—hundreds of colors and shapes; thousands upon thousands of candles snuffed far too soon. There were images of throngs of men and women visiting the quilt, holding each other through their grief as they celebrated and mourned friends, family, and lovers.

Tears were rolling down my cheeks before I thought to click out of the site. I wanted to look away, to see anything other than that eternal cloth, but I *had* to see it.

I had to see *them*. They deserved to be seen.

I grew up in the '80s, when AIDS first hit the news, but my life had been so sheltered and far removed from anything related to the gay community that I never grasped the magnitude of the tragedy. Dwayne said he'd lost several friends. I hadn't understood how that was possible at the time, how one person could know so many people to catch the same strange disease. It seemed such an odd coincidence. It didn't make sense.

The quilt *made* me see.

It made me see the vileness of a disease that struck down so many in the prime of life.

It made me see why Donny's eyes carried such fear and pain.

What it *didn't* do was help me know how *I* should feel or what I should do.

I was more confused than I had been before logging on, and definitely more so than at dinner. This was the '90s, but there was still so much unknown about AIDS. I knew unprotected sex was the primary way people got infected, but what about other activities? Donny and I hadn't done anything but kiss—and we'd done a lot of that. Could I have already been exposed? Did I need to go to a doctor? Could a negative guy even date a positive guy?

The ache of seeing the quilt fueled my fears and doubts. My breath became shallow as panic set in.

This *couldn't* be happening. I *couldn't* become a square on that quilt. My life was supposed to be more than a piece of cloth. I had no idea what it would become, but it was *supposed* to be more.

Without thinking, I logged off, sprinted to the den, and grabbed the phone. In two rings, Dwayne's sleepy voice answered. It was eleven thirty.

"Dwayne," I choked out between sobs. "I need to talk, please."

He didn't even ask why. "I'm on my way."

Everybody needs a Dwayne.

"WHAT HAPPENED?" DWAYNE ASKED AS I OPENED THE door. I was finally breathing again, but my eyes were puffy and rimmed with red. I probably looked like hell.

I didn't answer, just pulled him inside, shut the door, and wrapped my arms around his thin frame. He didn't resist the embrace, but it took him a moment to hug me back. I think he was shocked by the ferocity of my need. I really was a mess.

After a long moment standing just inside the doorway, we migrated to the den. I'd spent the thirty minutes it took him to arrive printing pages from all the sites I'd visited. They were splayed across the floor in front of the couch like a giant Japanese fan.

Dwayne scanned the papers, then his eyes widened and shot up to mine. "Michael, you're not—"

"Oh no. Not me."

His mouth quirked in concentration. "Donny?"

I nodded. The sobs I thought were sitting quietly in the corner returned, and Dwayne grabbed me again.

His presence calmed me quicker this time. When I pulled back, he stared at me with sympathetic, fatherly eyes. "Let's sit and talk."

I told him about dinner, and how the evening had ended with Donny, then about my online search. I showed him the images of horrific side effects and peppered him with a million questions. *Is Donny in pain? Will his belly do that? What about his cheeks? Will he get those sores? How long does he have?*

When I asked that last one, Dwayne's eyes spilled over.

"Michael, listen to me. HIV isn't the death sentence it once was. I lived through that time and, thankfully, never contracted the disease." He looked away and whispered, "Too many of my friends weren't so lucky."

Now it was my turn to sit back and watch as he relived a decade of loss.

I reached down and picked up the pages filled with images of the quilt. "I had no idea *so many*—"

"Yeah, *so* many." His voice was distant.

His shoulders slumped, and his eyes tightened as he fought off another wave. He sucked in a steadying breath and returned to the present.

"It's *not* like it was back then. We have great meds that keep the disease in check, and guys are living normal lifespans. Donny isn't going anywhere, and I want you to stop looking at websites and brochures that talk about side effects. Most of those are either rare or from a time before modern meds. They won't do anything but scare you."

I nodded weakly, relieved to have permission to discard those terrible pages.

"But…" I struggled with my next question. "What does it mean for Donny…and me? I mean, for *us*? He said it's why he wanted to wait for sex, so I would get to know him as a person before learning of his disease. He thought I might run away."

Dwayne nodded knowingly. "I've heard that a lot. He didn't want you to think he *is* his disease—but HIV is just something he deals with, like any other chronic illness."

"I guess that makes sense." I wasn't convinced.

He cocked his head. "If you'd known he was positive when you met, would you have dated him?"

"Of course. I mean…maybe. I…I don't know."

He let out a deep sigh. "Exactly—and you shouldn't feel bad about having doubts or questions. HIV has been a scary mystery since the whole thing started."

"I guess." I thought a moment. "But that still doesn't answer the question about Donny and me. I mean, can we date? Could we have sex? What about kissing or, I don't know, anything else?"

His eyes were so sad. It took him a long moment to respond.

"There are no absolutes. Think of the risk of infection as a scale. On one end, the riskiest thing you could possibly do would be to mix blood with blood. On the other end, you stay on opposite sides of the city and never stand in the same room."

The absurdity of his examples made me chuckle and lightened the mood. "Well, I don't think either of those options make sense."

His lips pursed into a tight smile. "No, probably not, but everything in between will either make you more or less likely to become infected—or, at least, exposed."

We spent the next few minutes talking through the litany of activities on Dwayne's scale of risk: kissing, licking, licking other things, kissing other things, putting other things in other places, and so on.

In the end, I knew a lot more about HIV, but was still baffled about dating Donny. My heart wanted to jump in my car, break a few speed laws, and wrap him in the biggest hug possible. I wanted to tell him it would all be okay, that we could make it work, that we could make *anything* work. I wanted to tell him I'd never run away from some stupid disease—and I certainly wouldn't ever run away from him.

I wanted all those things—at least, that's what my

heart wanted.

My head, never before one to interfere with my heart— or Little Michael—was ringing an alarm bell so loudly it hurt. It wouldn't be ignored. The *risk* was too great.

Risk.

Donny was a risk.

Dwayne watched me grapple with my thoughts in silence. He was good at giving me time to process. I wish he'd just given me answers, told me to stick it out or run away, one or the other, but I knew he wouldn't do that. He was too good a friend. I needed to come to terms with everything on my own, in my own time, otherwise whatever conclusions I reached wouldn't stick. I'd just be acting on *his* ideas and *his* decisions, not my own.

God, I hated being an adult.

"Am I an asshole?"

Dwayne looked up, brow furrowed. "In general? Or for something specific?"

Stupid friend, making me laugh again.

"For struggling with whether to keep seeing Donny. I mean…it's just a disease. It's not like he's a serial killer or anything. I wouldn't run from someone fighting cancer. It feels wrong somehow, all this questioning. Does that make me an asshole?"

"You're not an asshole—at least, not for this." He

smirked. "It makes you human. You said it yourself. A couple years ago, you didn't even know gays existed all around you, much less the dangers associated with this disease. Why should you feel guilty for being scared the first time you encounter it?"

"I guess. It still feels terrible. Donny's such a great guy."

"Great guys get sick too. And there are a lot of great guys out there who aren't a match for you."

My head snapped up. "Are you saying—"

"I didn't *say* anything. Donny may be perfect for you, or he might not be. You've known him for a few months. That's hardly enough time to place a lifetime bet, with or without the complications of HIV."

"Huh. Complications. That's one word for it."

He gripped my hand. "That's *exactly* what it is, a complication. It doesn't mean you can't be with him, but it does add to the list of things you need to think about when deciding who you spend your life with. It changes how you interact, how free you might feel with physical contact. Some guys will never be comfortable or get past that nagging voice in the back of their heads. Others are perfectly fine."

"I don't know where I am in all that."

"I know. Donny knows that too. It's what scares him."

Now my lips pursed. "Scared? Why would *he* be

scared? I'm not the one with the deadly virus."

Dwayne released my hand and slapped it reprovingly. "Don't be stupid. You're better than that. He's scared of *getting hurt*. He told you about other guys who ran away the minute they found out, and a lot of those were men he hadn't spent much time with, guys he didn't care about yet. He *cares* for you. If you ran, how do you think he would feel?"

I put my face in my hands. "This sucks so bad."

"Yeah, it does."

After another interminable moment, Dwayne reached across the couch and hugged me. It was two o'clock in the morning, and he looked exhausted. I felt drained.

"Don't make any decisions tonight, or tomorrow. Just take time to think. And whatever you do, don't look at those medical sites anymore. They tell you everything that *could* ever happen, not what's likely— or even reasonable—to happen."

I nodded and stood. "Talk tomorrow?"

"You bet."

THERE WAS NO BASKETBALL TO BE OFFICIATED THAT Monday night, so I went to the gym after work. My heart wasn't in it, but I walked through the motions anyway. I couldn't stop thinking about everything Dwayne had said the night before. As hard as I tried, I couldn't stop seeing the quilt.

Everywhere I looked, guys pulled or pushed, trying to get fitter or bigger or thinner. If a guy had even the slightest gut or sunken cheek, my brain flashed to those images of side effects. I couldn't stop it. The thoughts kept coming.

Frustrated, I racked my weights and left.

When I got home, I called Donny. I just needed to hear his voice. I hoped he wanted to hear mine.

"Hey," I said when he answered.

"Hey, yourself."

"How are the kids?"

"Fine. Frisky as always."

There was a long, awkward pause.

"You okay?" he asked.

"Oh yeah, I'm fine. Good. Really." *Idiot.*

"That's good." He didn't believe me. I could hear it.

"I missed your voice."

"Me too."

Another awkward silence.

"I need to feed the cubs. Chat later?"

"Sure," I said.

The tone that rang in the receiver when he hung up was like a heart monitor with a flat line.

5

—————

COLLEGE HUNKS MOVING JUNK

Donny and I never went out again.

We met at a local coffee shop one afternoon before his shift at the bar. I tried to meet his eyes, to explain how much I liked and admired him. Admired? I was such an idiot. Who says that?

Nothing made it better.

The tears clouding my eyes expressed more than any words could, and he gripped my hand. As I pulled away, he held me closer. He was such a good man. He didn't deserve my fear—but I couldn't reign it in. It had won.

In the years that would follow, I'd think back often to what could have been with Donny. What would life have held with the hunky bartender and his frisky cats? In our brief time together, he'd shown such tenderness and respect, such compassion. With each

33

memory, I knew I'd walked away from something special—no, from *someone* special.

When had life become so serious?

It was just yesterday I was fumbling my way out of a closet, laughing as I said and did stupid things borne out of sheltered ignorance or curiosity or some juvenile naivete. Now I was coping with life-threatening diseases and life-altering decisions, choosing paths in forked roads where only moments before I'd not even seen a road at my feet.

Why did life have to be so . . .

There wasn't a word for how my heart felt.

Dwayne and I visited him at the bar, and he was friendly and attentive, as always. He even had our drinks waiting before we could reach the bar from the front door. But he never asked me out again, and I never asked him. There was a sadness in his eyes each time we saw each other. I felt it in my own too.

Weeks turned into months of monotony at the new job. Years of schlocking drugs with my part-time preacher dad had taught me decent sales skills, and I was promoted to sales manager after only four months. I honestly had no idea what I was doing, but the previous sales manager left, and they needed someone to babysit the crazy sales dudes and translate programmer speak into English. It came with a raise, so I couldn't complain.

As shades of orange and yellow filled the trees, I became restless. I couldn't explain why, it was just a feeling that crept over me and wouldn't be ignored. Dwayne thought I was still smarting over Donny and just needed to get back on the horse—again. He'd been through a breakup with me before. He always shoved horses at me, and it usually worked. I'm a guy, after all.

This time, though, it didn't work. I needed something different, something *radically* different. I needed a change of scenery; a fresh start.

The more I thought about it, the more sense it made. I'd lived in Nashville my whole life. Hell, I could visit the room at Baptist Hospital where I was born. Outside of a few hundred-mile treks with the family for holidays to visit the grands, I'd never really left the county. Peter, the most amazing ab-covered roommate on the planet, had deserted me, and I was once again boyfriend-less. The idea of moving somewhere new was terrifying but exciting at the same time.

It was time for this baby bird to leave the nest. He needed to fly!

On a whim, I grabbed a map. From years of travel with my dad, I owned a stack of gas station maps— you know, the folding kind you could *never* neatly refold? My dad even bought me a road atlas detailing every interstate, street, and dirt path in the continental United States. That sucker was thicker than the Yellow Pages I'd let sit on my doorstep for two months.

I drew a circle in red around Nashville to narrow the search to within a few hundred miles. I figured if I hated the new place, missed the pack, or just wanted to move back, it made sense to be somewhat close to home base.

I knew I wanted to live in a bigger city, to experience the hustle and bustle I'd heard so much about, and that narrowed the hunt to a few large black dots and stars. Then I narrowed the choices to cities with large gay communities based solely on representation at softball tournaments my team had played in.

Yes, folks, I was downright scientific in my search for a new home.

At no point did cost of living, the job market, the housing market, traffic, or any other *logical* element factor in. This decision was based largely on how many teams a city sent to a gay softball tournament.

The leather-clad devil on my shoulder snickered as I narrowed the finalists to Atlanta and Chicago.

The angel began to cry.

I thought about Chicago. It was a musical. They liked pizza. That's about all I knew.

Atlanta was in Georgia, about an hour from where

my grandmother lived. The Braves were there. So were the Falcons, but nobody cared about them back then. I knew Atlanta had bad traffic, but had also hosted the Olympics. That's cool, right?

I remembered Chicago had the Cubs; again, not caring—possibly even less than I cared about the Falcons. Both teams sucked. Screw the goat and his curse.

Then it hit me. I *hated* cold weather.

Atlanta, here I come!

"I still can't believe you're doing this without finding a job first. How did you get an apartment?" Dwayne asked as I handed him my coffee maker.

"There was a Post Apartment down there. Since I'm already a resident, they considered it a transfer and didn't even ask about employment."

Dwayne laughed and shook his head. "This is either fate and you're blessed, or the dumbest thing I've ever seen. I'm still not sure which."

"Oh, stop it. Just be excited for me, old man. This will be an adventure!"

"You can say that again," he muttered, loud enough for me to hear.

The true test of friendship is if they'll help you

move. Dwayne had arrived early that morning, helped pack and haul every blender and box, cramming my U-Haul as fully as the sucker would allow. He'd taken several days off from the restaurant and was determined to drive down and get me settled in. He said he just wanted to see Atlanta, that it had been years since he'd visited "a real gay bubble," whatever that meant. I knew he just wanted to spend time together before our lives were irrevocably altered by time and distance. That part made me sad. I'd miss Dwayne more than any of the pack. He was my family.

Once the trailer was stuffed, we drove to do the same to ourselves at our favorite diner one last time. Katie was waiting for us as we walked in and practically threw herself at me. I almost choked on the scent of cheap perfume and bacon grease. Damn, I'd miss that too.

By three o'clock, we were on the road, Dwayne in my car and me in the U-Haul. Cell phones still weren't a thing yet, so we developed a honking and flashing lights system to let each other know when we needed to stop and stretch or pee.

Poor Dwayne and his itty-bitty bladder. The drive should've only taken four hours. We stopped six times.

By the time we pulled onto the Fruit Loop, also known as the Perimeter, it was dark. Dwayne had learned years ago never to trust my sense of direction, so I followed him into the city. Around nine o'clock, we pulled into my new apartment complex in a neighborhood called Midtown. A super-cute guard in a uniform shirt that was a size too small for his bulging arms greeted me, handed me my keys, and passed us through the gate. I caught him grinning in my rearview mirror as we drove through.

The Goddess of Delightful Dimples had definitely blessed this new land.

In that moment, I knew I'd *love* Atlanta.

6

___

WELCOME HOME

I was not born with decorating or nesting genes, so unpacking the U-Haul only took a few hours. Dwayne was an annoyingly early riser, so we started lugging suitcases and black trash bags full of clothes at an ungodly hour. Yes, I was a twenty-eight-year-old college student when it came to packing. My dear friend made fun of me the entire time.

Once everything was safely inside my third-floor abode, Dwayne set to work arranging my sparse collection of furniture. He spent a ridiculous amount of time scooching and scanning things in the den, rearranging the couch and cardboard box I used for a side table.

How could two pieces of furniture need that much attention? One of them wasn't even classified as furniture.

I'm a pretty simple guy in that regard. As long as I can see the TV from the couch and reach the kitchen in less than ten steps, I'm set. In the end, Dwayne moved everything back into design number seven and declared it perfect.

Around two o'clock, hunger overtook the excitement of pulling undies out of trash bags. Dwayne had heard of a place called Roasters that sounded remarkably similar to the rotisserie chicken restaurant we loved so much in Nashville, but neither of us knew where it was. On our way down the winding metal stairs, we heard splashing and laughter mixed with upbeat dance music booming from the complex's interior courtyard. That was as good a place as any to ask for directions.

Given the splashing, we deduced that a pool would be part of the scenery. (I know, we're still awaiting our Nobel Prize for that nugget of genius. Must've got lost in the mail.) What we hadn't expected was more than a hundred men swimming, drinking, laughing, and dancing. I would've bet every quarter in the sacred laundry stack that they were *all* gay. The kissing and playful touches gave that way. One didn't need a gaydar to peg this group.

Everywhere I looked, there were slabs of abs laying out for a tan, and most of the dudes were clad in little more than a sliver of cloth covering their pronounced dorsal fins.

Wait, that would be on their back, right? What's the other one called? Never mind. The point is, I could see lots of wee-wees and butts. It was awesome.

My keen powers of observation latched on to two things immediately. First, with over a hundred guys in thongs in the pool area, there was only one woman present. I knew Atlanta was supposed to be a gay-friendly town, but did straight people even live here?

Second, and even more remarkable, was the percentage of Hollywood Hotness splayed before us.

Let me explain. There are hot guys, and then there are the elite; the "Hollywood Hot." The difference is simple. A hot guy is your average handsome man you might find in any city across America. He could be muscular or thin, athletic or…you get the idea. Bottom line, he's widely regarded as handsome *in his town*.

Now, let's take that same handsome dude and drop him into the center of Hollywood. How does he compare? Let's face it, there's a difference between most next-door cuties and Henry Cavill.

Oh, Henry. You need me. You just don't know it.

Back to the pool.

Nashville had its share of beautiful, muscle-bound men. I would even say we had the average share of Hollywood Hotties too. Every city does. What stood before us at that pool made my heart thump harder than the bass thumping from the speakers. There were more genuine Hollywood Hotties contained in that gated gathering than I'd ever seen in one location, minus the Oscars or some other meeting of the elite.

"Where are we?" I asked Dwayne, unable to stop my eyes bouncing from one chest to the next.

"This is Midtown. You've moved into the Gay Bubble. Good luck."

He seemed unfazed by the buffet of buttocks before us—until a flock of very bubbly chickens showed up and stripped down to their banana hammocks. Dwayne nearly fainted. I was *sure* I heard his ankle bracelet buzz.

One of the chickens looked up from across the pool. He was a skinny blond twink barely into his twenties—*exactly* the kind of boy to rev Dwayne's engine. He tossed us a smile and wave, then turned and bent over to remove the pants he wore over his blue Superman speedos—the ones with the *S* logo on the center of his butt.

"We need to get directions and leave before I have heart failure," Dwayne said, dabbing sweat from his forehead.

I barked a laugh, then leaned over the railing to the

nearest sunbather. A few minutes and a dozen flirts later, we were headed to the parking lot.

"Have you moved into a gay bar?" he asked. "I knew Midtown was like Boystown in Chicago, but had no idea it was all *that*."

"Don't look at me. I've never been here before."

As we drove out of the complex, he started laughing for no apparent reason.

"Do I even want to know what you're laughing at?"

"Your apartment complex is called Monroe Place," he said between snorts.

"Uh, yeah. So?"

"I heard some of the guys back there calling it Melrose Place. It all makes sense now."

I didn't know what that meant, having refereed my way through nights filled with cheesy shows, but Dwayne laughed all the way to the restaurant.

WE WALKED INTO ROASTERS AND THE MOST DELICIOUS smell drifted into my nose. It was a combination of slow-roasted chicken and every vegetable I could imagine. The place itself was quaint, an upscale version of our diner back in Nashville. The patrons, however, were entirely *un*like anything I'd seen in our diner. We stood, gaping, in the doorway for a long moment, before a woman in her mid-sixties wearing a red-and-white checkered apron and tight bun waddled up.

"You boys here to eat or stare? You can do both at a table," she said without a hint of humor.

"Sorry, yes, we'd love a table. Thank you," Dwayne said.

There was one table open in a restaurant that seated one hundred, and it was all the way in the back by the kitchen. As we walked, weaving between tables, every head turned in a wave of glances.

Did I mention there wasn't a single woman in the place, other than Ms. Snarky Bun?

Every table we passed was filled with men. Young, old, tall, muscular, fat, thin…you name it. For every veggie on the menu, there was a flavor of gay to match it. There were athletic guys in T-shirts and tank tops who'd probably just worked out. One group of bespectacled boys was playing some weird board game with miniature dragons and knights. One of the nerds tossed a bunch of dice as we passed. They clearly represented an intellectual breed of gays I had yet to encounter and reminded me of the programmers I used to work with. A few booths held couples snuggled lovingly on the same side. They picked at each other's food. Most tables were filled with groups of three or four engaged in festive conversation.

It was all so delicious.

Uh, I mean…the food. The food smelled delicious.

Dwayne leaned across the table and whispered once Bun left, "Are we eating in a gay bar?"

I couldn't stop scanning the long room. My head was on a constant swivel, like a submarine periscope on the fritz.

The restaurant was twenty, maybe thirty yards wide, but a good Heisman-earning pass long. Booths lined either wall, and two rows of four-top tables filled the middle. Everything in the place was wooden, making it especially noisy when the gays got to gabbing. For the uninitiated, gays never actually stop gabbing. They merely pause to shove food—or other things—into their mouths.

Our table was crammed between the entrance to the kitchen and thin hallway that led to the restrooms. One particularly fit, handsome guy in a Lycra tank top slowed his stride as he passed us on his way to relieve himself. I looked up and he grinned, then continued on his way.

"I think I've died and gone to gay heaven," I said, staring after him down the hallway.

Dwayne chuckled and snapped his fingers. "I'm over here, Slutisha."

My head snapped around. "Hey! I've only lived here, what, fifteen hours? I haven't had time to earn that title. Give me a minute."

He rolled his eyes. "Based on the way you slept through Nashville's phone book, a minute is all it'll take before we'll have to move your worn-out ass to another city."

"Ha ha—"

I clamped my mouth shut, realizing a very amused, very cute young waiter was standing behind me, listening to the whole conversation. Dwayne had the nerve to wink at him. They'd conspired!

"Welcome to Roasters. I'm Jack. What looks good, gents?"

Sneaky Jack made his way to the side of the table so I could get a better look. My eyes darted between his dimples to his chest, then across his burgeoning arms.

"Uh-hum. Up here, gorgeous. I'm not on the menu tonight," Jack said with a smirk and a wink.

What was it with all the winking?

Dwayne spit the water he'd been sipping. "You'll have to excuse Michael here. He's fresh meat…I mean, he just moved here from Nashville."

"Aww. That's precious. Just a poor country boy on his first day in the big gay city," Jack said playfully, then winked again at Dwayne with a mischievous

gleam in his one open eye. "Let me handle the intro-
ductions."

I stiffened. Something was coming, I could feel it.

Jack turned, made a dramatic show of stuffing his
order pad in his apron, and clapped five times toward
the dining room. "Everyone! Hello! Attention down
here."

Someone decided to help and clanked a fork
against a plate several times, scaring the shit out of the
guy seated behind him. I laughed as the jumper turned
and glared at the clinker.

Once everyone had quietened and heads had
turned, Jack put a hand on my shoulder. "Gentlegays
of Atlanta, this is Michael. He just moved to Atlanta
and doesn't know a soul. And he's *purdy*." He drew
out the *purr* in purdy as he reached down and
squeezed my bicep. "Let's make him feel welcome,
alright?"

Everyone in the place, including Snarky Bun,
dropped their forks and applauded. Some hooted,
others hollered, a few yelled out phone numbers.

I'd never had a gay Quinceañera. I imagine that
moment was what it would feel like.

What does one do at such an auspicious event? I
didn't know whether to puff my chest out with pride
and wave like Miss America, or slink down the
hallway to hide in the bathroom.

Then again, maybe hiding in the bathroom when that many gay men had just been told to make me welcome wasn't the best idea.

Or maybe it was. I had a title to earn.

I sat and turned fifty shades of red. Not a sexy red, like in the *Fifty Shades* pleasure room. This was plain ole embarrassed red…all the way to the tips of my ears.

And that encouraged the mob.

Jack leaned down and kissed me on the cheek. The place erupted.

Dwayne, *former* best friend and wing man, had tears streaming down his cheeks as I squirmed under the rainbow spotlight.

Following Jack's instruction, every guy who passed our table on their way to the restroom paused and said some version of, "Hi, Michael. Welcome to Atlanta."

A few were a tad more forward. One was down-right lecherous. I got *his* phone number.

7

ON THE ROAD AGAIN

On my third day in Atlanta, I landed an interview for a sales manager gig at an IT staffing company. I didn't know anything about staffing, but had a decent understanding of the IT world and was pretty confident in my sales abilities. It was worth a shot.

My interviewer, Mark, was the outgoing sales manager. He wasn't leaving the company, he just didn't want to babysit the kids anymore. We laughed at that description. It was frighteningly accurate.

Thirty minutes into my chat with Mark, a rail-thin man waltzed into Mark's office. The guy was in his mid-thirties and was so pale he could've been an extra on *Buffy the Vampire Slayer*. I hopped to my feet and Mark introduced the newcomer as Ted, the company's founder and owner. We shook hands, spoke for five minutes, and he left.

In sales industry parlance, it was a drive-by. I hadn't been there an hour and knew an offer was about to hit the table.

It did. I was gainfully employed.

THE NEXT SUNRISE HERALDED MY FIRST SATURDAY IN Atlanta. We drove aimlessly, exploring my new town, pointing and chatting and laughing all the way. It was cool seeing the Olympic rings from when Atlanta played host to the world. The city experienced healthy growth before the Games, but exploded in the years that followed. Everywhere we looked, cranes towered atop partially completed buildings. Oddly, all that construction made the place feel alive, like the city itself was reaching up from the ground to spread new life everywhere.

I was surprised by how big the Braves' stadium was. They called it the Ted, for the illustrious Mr. Turner. Nashville didn't have a professional baseball team, so I'd never really been a fan, but I committed to buying some swag and learning more about my new team. When Dwayne asked if I planned to do the same with the Falcons, I laughed. I enjoyed winning a lot more than fitting in.

Margaret Mitchell's home was quaintly nestled amid Midtown's skyscrapers. I barely remembered seeing *Gone with the Wind*, but the author's house was a point on the tour I was glad we hit. Dwayne was thoroughly amused when I told him the house made me think about Carole Burnett wearing curtains with a rod spread across her shoulders.

Piedmont Park was almost as eye-popping as our first visit to Roasters. The park itself was impressively large and beautiful. On one side, sprawling, grassy fields were interrupted by softball diamonds and soccer goals. The other side held rolling hills with flat land in the center. Guys and gals cycled, skateboarded, and rollerbladed on the well-maintained walkways that encircled everything, while hundreds of other park-goers played frisbee with dogs, tossed footballs, or lounged in the sun.

The eye-popping part of our Piedmont Park drive-by was not in the number of Atlantans who'd ventured out to enjoy the fresh air, but in the makeup of the population there. Most of the guys were either shirt-less or wearing skimpy tank tops. Some snuggled on blankets, others hugged and kissed. When two groups met, they hugged like I'd seen so many times in the gay bars back in Nashville. Unlike the pool at Monroe

Place, there were quite a few women here. Some were in groups with the guys, but most were segregated in their own small huddles. Quite a few of the women wore some version of rainbow colors.

It was also notable that the Hottie Percentage held true. While other cities might boast a few truly beautiful among their flock, a solid plurality of those in Atlanta appeared to have broad, firm, very colorful feathers. My blood pumped a little faster, both at Little Michael's rising enthusiasm for the possibilities, and my heart's anxiety over just how intimidating all those tasty men were. How does one compete in a land of the truly blessed? The concentration of hotness was overwhelming.

That night, Dwayne took me out to celebrate getting a new job so quickly. I think we were both surprised how the fates appeared to be endorsing my move. We went to Roasters again. What can I say? We loved great chicken and veggies. The man meat on the menu didn't hurt either.

The festive gay vibe at dinner put both of us in the mood to tour a different side of Atlanta, so we grabbed one of the trusty *David* magazines from a rack at the front door and tried to guess which bar would be popular on a Saturday night. Dwayne ruled out a few places he remembered being either too seedy or aimed at a very specific niche within the gay community. I was no longer new to the rainbow world, but had yet to learn about different colored handkerchiefs and what tattoos meant when placed on the left or right arm. I made a mental note to return to the Gay Manual for guidance.

We settled on the bar with the largest ad, a place called Backstreet. Two whole magazine pages were filled with images of half-naked boys dancing on boxes or wiggling next to a bar. Every bartender pictured looked happy, hot, and horny.

No, I don't know how one *looks* horny in a magazine, but that's what I thought. Or maybe I was the one who—never mind.

Backstreet's parking lot rivaled that of the Connection in Nashville. Cars sprawled in every direction, while men poured out of them like ants headed back to their hill. As we pulled into a parking space, I felt butterflies I hadn't experienced since that first night I realized I had accidentally ended up in a gay bar.

I'd been to plenty of bars in Nashville since that night. Why was I suddenly nervous?

"Time for the big leagues." Dwayne answered my thoughts as we exited his car.

"Yeah. I'm actually a little nervous."

He barked a laugh. "That'll go away with the first

shake of your booty—maybe the first grab or pinch, if I remember your record in bars correctly."

I grinned. "It's more grabbable than pinchable. One might hurt one's fingers trying to pinch my granite cheeks."

"Gah!" He rolled his eyes and laughed. "Just don't leave me alone, alright? I have a feeling you'll be very popular. Fresh meat usually is."

"Aww. Meat. That's the sweetest thing you've ever called me."

He slapped my arm and playfully shoved me toward the bar entrance.

Over the next few hours, I counted a dozen chest strokes, two bicep squeezes, and more butt grabs than my alcohol-addled brain could remember. Dwayne cackled as I nearly jumped out of my painted-on jeans with the first few flirts—but I settled in and came to enjoy the attention I'd never received as a freckled, ginger young nerd. Even some of the Hollywood Hotties gave me a respectable ogle. Who knew? I might actually have a shot in this land of lovelies!

Dwayne pulled me away from a tall, hunky, curly-haired boy whose nipples shown bright red in the strobing lights. I hadn't realized pinching nipples was nearly as popular as gripping butt-cheeks. I reluctantly gave Naughty Nips a peck on the cheek and allowed myself to be dragged out to the car. Dwayne was a blast to hang out with, but his tolerance for watching me flirt with every dude with dimples lasted only so long.

———

THE NEXT DAY, DWAYNE RETURNED HOME. AS MUCH as we liked to tease each other, it was a sad parting. We offered all the promises friends make when moving hundreds of miles away from each other, pledging to keep in touch and stay just as close as we'd always been, but we both knew life didn't work that way. Despite our best intentions, he would get busy chasing chicken and trying to remove his ankle bracelet, and I would start a new life exploring my new city and job.

We were about to drift, and I *hated* it.

I hugged him so long, he had to tell me to let him go. Then he did something he'd never done in all the time we'd known each other. He reached up and kissed me on the cheek, then rubbed it with his fingers. My heart stuck in my throat. I knew he was saying goodbye, being a loving, caring friend, but I didn't want to let go.

Watching him drive through the gates of Monroe Place, a part of me left Atlanta.

8

THINK!

I owned two suits. They hung, side by side, on the back of my closet's folding doors. A dozen or so ties lay scattered across the bed as I held each one up in a desperate attempt to pick my first-day-on-the-new-job outfit. I'd never been good with that sort of thing, and starting a new job hadn't magically imbued me with better fashion sense. I picked a white shirt, charcoal suit, and blue tie with tiny pink dots. I had no idea if it matched.

A mug of coffee and a twenty-minute drive later, I stood in the lobby of my new office. A girl who'd clearly had more coffee than I greeted me with a chipper smile. She sat behind a massive cherry-red unit that rose nearly to my chest. On the wall behind her, highlighted with bright spotlights, was the company's name in silver metal letters: Think!. I later learned they rarely used the second word in the name, *Resources*, because the owner liked how catchy Think! was.

When the receptionist learned I was the new sales manager, she hopped up from her seat behind the sprawling switchboard and shook my hand. Somehow, her highly caffeinated smile widened. It looked painful.

Seconds later, a towering form filled the entry to the right of the reception desk. Mark must've been walking by when I arrived because the girl hadn't had time to call for him. He smiled, stretched out his meaty paw, and gripped my hand like he was juicing an orange.

"You have no idea how glad I am you're here," he said.

I wasn't sure how to read his enthusiasm, but I tried to match the firmness of his grip and the tone of his voice. I smiled up at the giant. "I'm happy to be here."

"Come on back. I'll give you the tour, then you can get settled into your office. There's a team meeting at nine to introduce you. No pressure, but they're a tough crowd."

We strode past a small grouping of cubicles filled with programmers and clerical staff. Mark pointed to my office opposite this cluster. It was about what you'd expect, a twelve-by-twenty box with a desk, credenza, bookshelf, and two chairs for visitors. The back wall was entirely glass overlooking a grassy field. I noted the blank walls and desk, wondering how I'd make the place my own.

The office beside mine sat empty. Mark explained it was for the manager of the recruiting teams. I had no idea what that meant, but nodded thoughtfully. He explained I would have a heavy vote in who was hired for that role.

I added 'learning what the hell a recruiting manager was' to my growing list of homework.

Mark's corner office sprawled across one end of the building, taking up enough space to fit three offices the size of mine. Apparently, he was an IT staffing baller. Dennis, the head of technology, hopped up from his chair and greeted me as we passed his closet-sized space.

"Hey, you must be the new sales manager. Michael, right?"

I nodded and shook his hand. His grip was decidedly looser than Mark's—and slimier. It felt a little like squeezing a snake that wanted desperately to slither away.

"Great. We're glad you're here. Don't touch the computer until I show you how to log in and have given you the welcome speech, okay?"

I glanced at Mark. He rolled his eyes just enough for me to see.

"Uh, sure. I'm not that great with computers anyway. I could use any help you can give me."

"Great. Just don't push buttons or click anything you don't understand. Okay?"

"Deal."

Mark's paw nudged my arm, a hint meant to save me. I took it gratefully.

"Nice meeting you, Dennis. See you after the sales meeting," I said, and Mark and I began moving further down the hall. Dennis's door clicked shut.

Mark leaned down and whispered, "He means well, and he's a hell of an IT guy, but he's kind of a dick."

As the new guy, I wasn't sure how to react to Mark's frankness, but chuckled and gave him a tight smile. "Need to win him over. Got it."

The last office we visited was that of the owner, Ted, who sat glaring at one of five computer screens spread across his insanely long desk. He didn't notice when we walked in and Mark had to clear his throat twice to get him to look up.

"Oh, Michael, are you starting already?" he said, clicking a few keys before making his way around the Tajima desk.

Mark saved me a second time. "Today's Michael's

first day. He meets the troops at nine. I can't wait to pass this baton."

Ted grinned and nodded, as though they'd had that conversation a hundred times. "Welcome. Why don't you have a seat, and I'll tell you a little more about our company, then you can go settle into your office. I assume Dennis beat you over the head about the computer already?"

Mark coughed a laugh from behind me.

I nodded. "Yes, he pretty much told me to wait for instruction before touching anything."

Ted smirked. "Good. Don't believe his bluster, he's a good guy. We had a bad hack a year ago and he's paranoid now. That's probably healthy for an IT manager these days."

The three of us sat at a small conference table, where Ted and Mark described the company's founding and growth. The pair alternated, often finishing each other's sentences like an old married couple, but appeared annoyed when it happened— again, like an old married couple. They were forthright and friendly, but serious about their business. Mark loved the sales side and wanted nothing more than to focus on his own personal hunt for new clients. Ted wanted to turn Think! into the largest IT recruiting firm in the country. He spoke passionately about the computers and process, how the website drove traffic for new candidates and winnowed them down for the perfect hire.

Months later, replaying that conversation in my mind, I realized the one thing Ted didn't talk about—not even once—was the *people* who worked for him.

MY FIRST WEEK WAS FILLED LARGELY WITH MEETINGS with each member of my new sales team. I now oversaw thirty-two men and women, most of whom were in their twenties or early thirties. The one-on-one meetings were interesting. Virtually every person who walked into my office did so with an air of caution, as if unsure whether they were meeting an ally or executioner. I dedicated most of the time to asking questions about their background, interests, and goals for the future. I'd learned long ago that nothing calms a salesperson more than the sound of their own voice.

The recruiting team was slightly larger than my sales team, boasting forty-five members. I pitied whoever we hired for that management gig. My group was overwhelming as it was, I couldn't imagine trying to wrangle an additional thirteen people.

On Thursday, Ted's head popped into my office. The rest of him snaked around the wall. He was an odd man.

"We have candidates for the other manager position we'd like you to interview. You free at two this afternoon?"

I scrolled through my calendar, then nodded. "I'm free. Anything in particular you want me to look for?"

He shook his head. "No. Just trust your gut. This person will be your partner in running the teams, so we need you to be comfortable with whoever we hire."

Without another word, he vanished, leaving me staring at the empty doorway.

WHEN TWO O'CLOCK ROLLED AROUND, I FOUND MY way into the conference room where the first candidate waited. He was a tall, thin, extremely pale man with tight-cropped black hair and brown eyes that bugged out like a pug's. I tried not to stare, but he blinked rapidly when he talked and made it impossible to look away. The effect was both comical and creepy.

Pug Man had never worked in sales. He'd never led a team. He had no experience with recruiting, and barely any experience working in a professional setting. I wasn't sure why the recruiters had moved him through to the interview stage, as his résumé clearly mirrored the vacant look in his far-too-pronounced eyeballs. I made a note to discuss filter criteria with the recruiting team.

At two thirty, the receptionist appeared and announced my next interview had arrived.

Next interview? I was sure Ted had only mentioned one.

Nevertheless, I thanked Mr. Pug, then asked Perky Patty to show him out and bring in the next victim.

Candidate number two was a woman with gray hair pulled into a tight bun. She wore a sharp black pant suit with a frilly white blousy thing puffing out the front.

I'm *sure* that's what it's called. Stop snickering.

As she entered the conference room, she extended a stiff, unyielding hand and pursed her lips into a taut, thin line I took for a smile. I quickly learned it was *not* a smile. Herr Hilda did not know *how* to smile. She spoke in short, clipped sentences, with the precision of a surgeon's scalpel. I felt each cut—I mean, word—deeply. Unlike Mr. Pug, her eyes never blinked, never wavered, never left mine. Strong eye contact was a great quality in a professional, but hers was unnerving. I kept waiting for the creepy music to start so I could run to safety into the cemetery or barn filled with chainsaws. Wasn't that always the safest place to run in a scary movie?

At three o'clock, my salvation in the form of the

doorknob squeaking open arrived. Perky Patty appeared and announced the third candidate's turn. That was both a relief and annoying. I couldn't wait for Herr Hilda to leave, but again, I was not expecting this many interviews. How long would this day last? And how bad would the candidates get? I hoped this wasn't the quality of candidates we put in front of our clients.

I asked Patty to stall the next candidate so I could check my calendar and move any conflicts. Thankfully, all I had was another training session with Dennis on how not to break his network. He gladly rescheduled.

Candidate number three was ushered into the room roughly ten minutes past the scheduled start time. Patty introduced the woman as Constance Black, then closed the door as she left.

"Constance, I'm so sorry to keep you waiting. Today's been back-to-back," I said, stepping forward, hand extended.

"Please, call me Connie. You gave me time to grill Patty. She's delightful."

Connie was pleasant, professional, and I was immediately drawn to her easy smile.

"Hope she said nice things," I quipped.

"Oh, she did. Not about you, but about the company."

"So, she said bad things about me?" I raised a brow.

She grinned. "I wouldn't say *bad* things. Let's just say the jury's still out on the new guy."

She was teasing me, in an interview—an interview that had barely begun. I didn't know whether to be offended or impressed, but her confidence and openness was refreshing, and I couldn't help but like her.

We talked for over an hour, lobbing questions back and forth with the comfort of old friends. Connie loved working with people, developing them, finding what made them tick, and using that knowledge to help them succeed. She didn't have direct recruiting experience, but had led several teams in other industries. I was confident she'd pick up the recruiting business quickly. By the time Patty appeared to check on us, Connie and I were leaning forward across the table, giggling like schoolmates at some story about a former employee.

Ted made me interview two more people the next day, but Connie was the clear winner. She was sharp, well-spoken, endearing, and, most of all, she made me laugh. It was a match made in corporate heaven.

9

DEBUTANT

Friday after work, I decided it was time to find a new gym. The muscle buffet on display at the pool had made it clear I had work to do. I was in great shape for Nashville's quaint gay scene, maybe even in the top third of contenders, but I was merely average in the sea of hotness that was Atlanta.

I turned to the literary reference material that had proven most effective in guiding me thus far—*David* magazine. Using Dwayne's flawless logic, I found the gym with the largest ad. A quick three-minute drive from Monroe Place, nestled in a residential valley in Midtown, was Powerhouse, gym to the gay stars—or, at least, the boys who lived in Midtown. There were a few other options, but they weren't as close by and didn't show up as prominently in *David*.

"Welcome to Powerhouse," a deep, friendly voice

rumbled as I entered. I looked up to find an enormously muscled guy standing behind a counter. He wore a white tank top with Powerhouse printed in bold red lettering across the chest. He was clearly a bodybuilder, as muscles I couldn't identify bulged out of every opening in his shirt. I swear his neck was wider than his head. I tore my eyes from his eighty-inch arms and read his name tag.

"Hi, uh, Greg. I'm looking for a gym to join."

"Awesome." He grabbed a clipboard and handed it to me. "Fill out that guest pass info. I'll give you the tour."

A few minutes into our tour, I realized I had even more work to do than I'd thought. Everywhere I looked, perfectly sculpted men pulled and pushed, stretching already rippling muscles past their limits. Rows of guys lay on blue foam pads, stretching legs and working abs. I saw more abs in that ten-minute tour than I think I'd seen in my whole life.

Sweet baby Jesus.

I followed Greg through an entryway that wound around an S-shaped wall then opened into the locker room. I nearly missed a step. A dozen naked gods strutted about the room. A few wore towels tied about their waists, but most seemed pleased with the opportunity to display their, um, hard work. And some of their, um, *work,* was definitely hard. I caught my face in the mirror and realized my mouth was open and eyes were bugged out, darting faster than a squirrel crossing a road. Greg laughed, snapping me out of my daze.

"Lockers over there. Showers to the right. Steam room and hot tub are in the back. This side is men only, so the hot tub and steam room are clothing optional."

I'd stopped listening as a particularly hot guy emerged from the shower and exercised the *optional* part of that policy. My head followed as he passed, and I stumbled into Greg, who'd stopped to show me something.

"Oh, Greg, sorry. I, uh, tripped over a towel."

He laughed again. "You're new to Atlanta, aren't you?"

I nodded sheepishly.

"You'll be fine. It takes a little getting used to. I've lived here over twenty years, wouldn't want to be anywhere else." He eyed my body. "Looks like you've been working out. Chest is filling out, arms are nice. What are your fitness goals? Do you know where you'd like to see your body?"

The hottie from the shower walked by and made eye contact over Greg's shoulder.

"I, uh, goals, well…I, uh…"

"Let's go back to the desk. It might be easier to

talk out there." He chuckled to himself as we walked back up front. I felt every eye in the place follow me. Should I have been proud? Were they *liking* the new guy? I felt like I was trying out for some team and didn't even know what sport we were playing.

Greg finished the enrollment process and sent me out the door with a shiny new key fob to scan each time I worked out. I know it sounds silly, but there was something about that plastic hanging off my keyring that made me feel like I really lived here now. I was officially an Atlantan.

I GRABBED SOME CHINESE TAKEOUT ON THE WAY BACK to my apartment, unsure what to do with my first weekend alone. After a plateful of cashew chicken and white rice, I turned to my trusty *David* for guidance. *David* and I were becoming great friends.

The bars were listed in two places. Ads were splashed throughout the magazine, displaying bartenders and bar-goers in various states of drunken delight. Some were specific in their marketing, showing guys in cowboy hats and fringe shirts, indicating the bar that catered to country-loving gays. Another showed large, hairy men in black studded leather. One guy held a chain attached to a collar encircling another dude's neck. I wasn't entirely sure what Disney theme that represented, but knew it wasn't what I was looking for.

What was more interesting than the themes in the ads was the specificity with which they advertised which night was best to visit. Backstreet and the Armory, two of the larger bars that happened to share a parking lot, stressed Fridays and Saturdays. The leather lads represented The Heretic, which noted Wednesday nights were their specialty. Other, more generally themed locations claimed Mondays and Thursdays.

Sundays were apparently all about a tea dance. I had no idea what a tea dance was. The ad even had a picture of a tea bag in a shot glass with its little white tag dangling over the side. Did gays have a special thing for tea? Were all gays now British? I was baffled —and more than a little intrigued.

In addition to the weird tea reference, that particular dance started at two o'clock in the afternoon. Virtually no one showed up to any of the bars before midnight, but that major weekly event started in the middle of the day. The whole thing seemed odd.

Tuesdays appeared uniquely devoid of bar mayhem. Even gays had to rest from all their merriment, I supposed.

Research complete, I closed the lid on my leftover

Chinese food and decided to check out the bar of the day—or night, as was the case on a Friday. It was only nine o'clock, far too early to go out, so I flipped on the TV and watched *Star Trek* reruns until the witching hour arrived. As excited as I was to venture out, I forced myself to wait until twelve thirty to get ready.

One mustn't appear too eager, must one?

I squeezed into my look-at-my-ass jeans, threw on a nearly clean white T-shirt, and headed out. Backstreet called to me again, and I felt a flurry of something in my gut as I looked at the ad for the address. If the percentage of Hollywood Hot held true from what I'd seen in town so far, this was going to be eye-candy heaven, but also I worried I was out of my depth. How could a raised-by-wolves preacher's kid from small-town Nashville fit into this big city sea of hotness?

I PULLED INTO THE MASSIVE PARKING LOT A QUICK five minutes later. The Armory's squatty long building sat at one end, while Backstreet's multi-floored monstrosity consumed the side perpendicular to the Armory. Scowling security guards attempted to direct the flow of cars, but were unable to prevent them from stacking up beyond the entrance. It took twice as long to park as it had to drive from my apartment.

Men in twos and threes, mostly in jeans and T-shirts or tank tops, laughed and squealed their way into the bars. As I walked past one group, a young guy with wild blond hair styled in the popular finger-in-a-light-socket motif scuttled away from his pack and pinched my butt. I nearly leapt out of my jeans, and the dumbfounded expression on my face when I turned around sent blondie's whole group into a fit of laughter. I stared, stunned, as they *skipped* toward Backstreet's doors.

The Connection in Nashville was immense. Its main dance floor held five hundred, and each of the smaller bars held many hundreds more. The first few times I went there, it was both thrilling and dizzying. To see so many gay men packed into one place was beyond anything familiar to me. While Backstreet packed in hundreds of men, probably more than a thousand, it had a completely different vibe. All the basics were there: bars at every turn with half-naked, totally hot bartenders, boxes on which scantily clad men danced, and multiple levels allowing lurkers and lurkees to do whatever it is they do in the dark. The general age was twentysomething, similar to Nashville's bar scene.

But there were also clear differences.

The Atlanta boys did not disappoint. The intimidating ratio of Hollywood Hot to Normal Hot was off the chart. I'd never seen so many muscles and pearly whites under one roof. In Nashville, I could stand in my safe, dark corner and pick out those who deserved a Best in Show ribbon. Just like in dog shows, where hundreds entered the competition, only a few walked away with the honors. Backstreet followed different judging criteria. Ridiculous hotness surrounded me, pressing and shoving, dancing and swaying. Every time I thought I'd found the vaunted Best in Show, some other stunning specimen would walk off the cover of his magazine and into the bar. It was mesmerizing.

Another difference was something we'll call the IKEA Effect. There wasn't really a conscious flow of traffic, and it was easy to lose yourself in the maelstrom as you…um…browsed. At the Connection, there were obvious wide hallways that led from one section to the next. Backstreet had none of that organization. Men squeezed and squirmed, headed in every direction. Even the entrance held that fighting-against-the-current feeling, as departing guys shouldered new arrivals in a contest of wills.

Backstreet was also darker than the Connection. Sure, when strobes were flaring and the dance floor was rocking, both bars had dim lighting, but Backstreet lacked the towering ceiling of the Connection, making it feel more closed, and somehow more intimate.

It took an hour for me to identify the final, most important difference: guys in Nashville made eye contact and were generally friendly. These newer, hotter models seemed intent on some mission—or on being the object of someone else's mission, I wasn't sure which. They rarely made eye contact, and when they did, it was often followed by a 'what are you looking at?' scowl. Did pretty people not want to be ogled? Apparently, the rules were different in Atlanta. The Gay Manual had failed to prepare me properly.

I ogled anyway. Screw them.

Not literally.

Well, maybe…

Midway through the night, I was standing in line for the restroom when a guy sidled up beside me. He bobbed a tad faster than the beat of the music, twitching more than dancing. His eyes were wide and unfocused. I took a step forward as someone left the restroom.

"Hey." Twitchy's voice was as twitchy as his dance moves.

"Uh, hey."

"You want some coke?"

I cocked my head and held up my plastic cup, half full of brown fizzy goodness. "I'm all set, thanks."

He stopped twitching and gave me that sideways head flop a dog gives when asked a question, as if he couldn't fathom the meaning of what I'd said. His eyes managed to focus and held the same confused expression as his head tilt.

I rattled the ice in my cup. "Coke. I'm still half full—but thanks."

He got it, then started laughing. I still don't know what I said that was so funny. He gave me one last look, shook his index finger accusingly, then disappeared into the crowd.

Atlanta guys were weird.

10

CURIOUS GEORGE

As the weeks rolled by, I fell into a comfortable routine. Think! didn't open the doors until eight thirty, so my anti-morning-person nature was well pleased. Connie got the recruiting manager gig, and she quickly became my new best friend. We collaborated well on projects while each learning the ropes of our new position. It was fun figuring it out together. Aside from our shared brain in working with teams, Connie had an infectious laugh—and she laughed all the time. Barely a day passed that we weren't giggling like children over some silliness.

After work, I drove directly to the grocery store to purchase my pre-workout snack, a single Fuji apple. The first time I set my lonely fruit on the conveyor belt, the checkout clerk's eyes drifted from the apple to me, then back to the apple.

"Just an apple?" she asked, her voice straddling curiosity and amusement.

I nodded, glancing at her name tag. "Yes, Miss Anne. Just the apple."

By my third visit, Anne had come to expect my odd purchase and welcomed me by name.

My workout began with fifteen minutes of cardio to wake me up from Think!ing all day, and rotated between chest and biceps, back and triceps, and the dreaded leg day. I did twenty minutes of abs after each lifting session, then another thirty minutes of cardio on the elliptical. Workouts lasted roughly two hours. By the time most workouts finished, I was mentally and physically exhausted and hungry enough to eat all the apples Anne might have stashed in the storeroom.

Cooking had never been my strong suit. Moe's, the nearby takeout Chinese place, and a Western-novel-themed restaurant called Cowtippers usually won my post-workout business. Aside from the fun name, I especially liked Cowtippers' wooden patio with dozens of outdoor tables where traffic, both driving and pedestrian, were visible. What dinner didn't go well with eye candy?

As I sat eating my sweet potato drenched in brown sugar and cinnamon goodness, I decided to find out what Atlanta had to offer beyond the bar scene. Once again, *David* turned out to be helpful, offering pages of activities run by various local gay groups. I had thought we were lucky because Nashville had a decent softball league and a pickup volleyball night, but as I flipped through page after page, I was awed by the breadth of Atlanta's community. There were groups for *everything*.

God bless the boys and girls in the Atlanta Gay Quilters and Atlanta Rainbow Chess Society. Everyone needs a home, even nerds with needles.

I circled the contact information for the softball and volleyball leagues—they had a whole volleyball *league*, not just a pickup night. After my head-spinning, scantily clad introduction that first day at the pool, I hadn't thought my love for Atlanta could deepen. I'd never known there were cities where I could be around gay people and not feel the need to look over my shoulder, to wonder who might be watching. Don't get me wrong, I loved living in Nashville—it was an amazing, growing town with some of the nicest people on the planet—but the idea of two men or two women holding hands as they strolled down Broadway was unimaginable. I was never worried about being attacked, but growing up in the buckle of the Bible Belt did give a preacher's kid a unique appreciation for the power of excommunication.

Staring at the pages of Atlanta's most colorful

organizations, I realized how amazing my new home really was.

THE RHYTHM OF THE BAR SCENE BECAME PART OF MY routine. I didn't go out much during the week, largely because going to a bar before midnight was a waste of time and I needed my beauty sleep on school nights. But I looked forward to Friday and Saturday nights, and whatever mischief they might bring. On my fifth weekend in the City of the Peach, I decided to be adventurous and visit one of the darker-themed bars, The Heretic. Even the name made me shiver with excitement.

My little devil appeared in his tightest leather, a wide grin spread across his miniature face. "Dude, it's about time. You're gonna love the dark side," he said with a glee I didn't know devils could possess.

"I'm just going to visit, to walk through and see what it's like, then I'm leaving for the safety of Blake's."

The devil actually coughed a laugh, and I swear I felt spittle on my neck. "You are not a *stand-and-model* gay. You're a *seize him by the balls and do nasty things to him* gay—or a *tie me to the bedpost with your silk*—"

"Hey!" I protested.

"Blake's is a perfectly fine place to see hot guys walking back and forth or…holding up walls."

Man, he was bossy, but he had a point. Blake's was full of pretty boys who wouldn't do much more than stand around. On the other hand, the thought of exploring uncharted territory made my pulse race— and made Little Michael tingle. Maybe I'd stay at The Heretic for a half hour. It deserved a fair shot, right?

"You bet your ass strap, it does!" The devil clapped his hands together and a puff of dark smoke wafted past my ear. "And next week we'll try The Eagle or Bulldogs!"

The Eagle? Bulldogs? I didn't remember seeing either of those particular tourist attractions advertised in my trusty *David*. I'd have to do more research before agreeing to that adventure, as something in his voice made me question the Sunday School-esque nature of those establishments.

MIDNIGHT ARRIVED AND SEXY JEANS WERE DONNED. The time had come for my virgin voyage to The Heretic.

My nerves fluttered once again, so I hung out in the parking lot and watched the boys walk toward the entrance to get a feel for the place. This was a decidedly different crowd than the one I'd seen at Armory and Backstreet. A fair number of the guys were big— and I don't just mean tall. If the check boxes ranged from short to tall, skinny to plump, and muscular to athletic, The Heretic's crowd was weighted toward the heavier, hairier side. The median age was also older, somewhere in the thirties, versus the twentysomethings who dominated the other bars.

Even the sounds coming from the groups of men were different. Where many of the gaggles at Backstreet giggled their way into the building, deep, rumbling bass tones echoed across the paved lot here.

Backstreet had a young, sexy, hot vibe.

The Heretic felt *manly*.

While Backstreet boys begged to be worshipped, men at The Heretic looked like they'd rather shove you against the wall and make you their—

Anyway.

The Heretic also had a thing for leather. Black, brown, blue—yes, there were men in blue-tinted leather—no one seemed to care as long as you wore it. Many of the more muscular guys wore leather vests without a shirt, giving you a tasty hint of what lay beneath without fully revealing their deliciousness. Others opted for harness things I'd seen on dogs at the park the other day. A few even had a collar with a tag.

Images of walking through Nashville Zoo with Donny streaked through my mind, but this was a *very* different kind of zoo. Instead of big cats and elephants, I watched a parade of bears, otters, and other critters I didn't yet recognize stroll by.

A massive guy in leather chaps—and no pants underneath—walked by carrying a silver leash attached to a studded collar fastened around the neck of a young skinny dude shuffling sheepishly behind. I wasn't sure if the follower actually wanted to be there, until he suddenly perked up, bounded forward two strides, and licked his master's ear.

I couldn't stop staring. My dog used to do that to me.

We definitely weren't in Nashville anymore.

A good fifteen minutes passed before I pulled myself up by my balls and climbed out of my car. I hadn't noticed the giant circular sign on the wall beside the door until then. It was black with the name of the club wrapped around the outer edge in white. The image of some bird of prey with ears and a long tongue stared down at me from the sign's center.

Now I really was nervous.

"Just you, precious?"

My head snapped forward. A snow-topped, rail-thin man behind a high-top table blinked and smiled.

"Uh, yeah. Just me."

"Five bucks," he said, hand extended.

A cover charge. That was new.

The guy gripped my arm with his outstretched hand and leaned over the table. "You've never been here, have you?"

I shook my head.

He chuckled. "Go on in. Tonight's on me. Just don't stop walking if you go into the back hallway. They'll eat a pretty little thing like you alive."

I nodded nervously and hurried past, but froze at a wall lined with men that forced me to go left or right. The men grinned as my head snapped skittishly back and forth. Finally, one of them took pity on the scared little rabbit and said, "Left is leather and military, right is sports."

I darted right faster than they could laugh.

The sports bar was the size of a two-bedroom apartment without walls. The only sign of sports of any kind was a lone television tuned to ESPN. I laughed at the absurdity of professional bowling playing in a seedy gay bar on a Friday night.

And just like that, my nerves eased.

I took a deep breath and looked around. Most of the sports crowd were younger, leather-less guys, with just a smattering of leather caps and vests thrown in for seasoning. There wasn't nearly as much space here, so every step meant rubbing shoulders and chests. I said a polite "excuse me" each time I bumped into someone, until a dude turned around, ran both hands down my chest, and said, "You're excused. Now do that again."

My mouth fell open. A friend of Mr. Hands stepped around him and grinned. Before I knew what was happening, his meaty palm was rubbing up and down my jeans, hungrily hunting for Little Michael. Startled, I jumped back and nearly caused a tumbling domino effect of dudes. The guy behind me wrapped both hands around me, gripping my abs and pulling me into him. Meanwhile, Meaty Palm decided a massage was in order. Mr. Hands reappeared and reached around to squeeze my butt.

Three guys I didn't know in the middle of a bar were rubbing and squeezing me, and I couldn't stop it—didn't stop it; didn't *want* to stop it—and then a barback carrying a case of beer stepped between us and freed me from their grip.

"Coming through. Everyone back." He turned to me as the sea parted. "You okay?"

I tried to play it cool. "I'm…uh…I'm good. Yeah. Really. I'm great."

His smile was thin. "I'm Jase. Ask for me if you have any trouble, okay?" Then he stepped to the bar and heaved his case of beer through the swinging door.

When I turned back, Mr. Hands and Meaty Palm had vanished. I squeezed back to the entrance and out the door without looking back. I climbed into my car, reveling in the comfort and safety of her well-worn seats, and calmed my breathing. I wasn't sure why I was so terrified. Guys had grabbed my ass before and I'd bragged about it to Dwayne. The men in The Heretic weren't exactly ripping my jeans off, but their touch felt more like a violation. I didn't understand why.

The weirdest part of it all was the reaction of the guys packed around us. Except for my savior, Jase, none of the others seemed bothered in the least. I wasn't exactly thinking clearly in the moment, but I remembered several men glaring and grinning at the display of wanton sexuality before them—and that was in the *sports bar*. The doorman warned me about some back hallway, not the bar areas. How much more handsy would that stretch of darkness be?

Puff. The devil was back, now in a road-worn, black biker's jacket and faded torn jeans.

"Dude, you're such a *puss.* The only way to know is to go back in there and see for yourself—or feel for yourself, if the mood hits ya."

I didn't like the way he chuckled, so I flicked him

off my shoulder like a wayward bug. He vanished in another puff of black vapor as his leather-clad body slammed into the car window.

"Oof! Your loss—" was the last thing I heard before starting my car and heading home.

11

VIRTUAL REUNION

My dreams were filled with images of men in leather, men taking off leather, men swinging leather over their heads, men putting leather on me, and on it went. I tossed in my sleep as hands reached from every direction. Fingernails grazed my bare flesh. Strong fingers gripped me, rubbed my back and legs and butt, stroked my—

I woke up drenched in sweat. Terror had taken a back seat to intrigue and a heart-thumping *something* I couldn't identify—but it felt exactly like the thrill I remembered from my night a few years ago with Fly Boy and his silk ties.

Fear mingled with desire wrapped in pleasure.

Yeah, that summed it up.

I'd never been a fan of cold showers, but one seemed

highly appropriate that morning. Once the shock of the cold subsided, it felt good to wash The Heretic off and return my brain to some semblance of normalcy. The devil didn't reappear, but I thought I heard the tinkle of faint laughter coming from the angel's side of my brain.

Great, now they were *both* amused.

After a quick breakfast of toasted blueberry bagel with strawberry cream cheese, I refilled my mug with java and strode back into the bedroom to check email and kill some time chatting on AOL. A few new Nigerian princes were offering me large sums of money. They were really nice people, but I felt guilty taking their money for nothing, so I replied, suggesting they give it to charity.

Email complete, I remembered wanting to check out the Eagle and Bulldogs online. The devil seemed determined to expose me to every facet of Atlanta. His suggestions were usually fun, but came with some wicked twists.

While I waited for the Eagle's painfully slow website to pull up, something flashed in the corner of the screen: one of my friends was online.

RAL2027.

Huh. The screen name was vaguely familiar, but it had been months since we last chatted—and in AOL time, that was decades. I'd printed hundreds of profile sheets since chatting briefly with that dude, and my online memory sucked.

HEY, HAVEN'T SEEN YOU IN A WHILE.

I was a little surprised when he IMed me. I quickly flipped through my overstuffed notebook of profile sheets to review my notes on this mysterious candidate.

All his profile listed were the standard stats: *SWM, 31, 5'9, 170, 31w, 16a, 8c.*

Beneath the printed line, I had written, "Ryan. Seems nice. No pic."

It didn't look like we'd had much of a conversation—at least, none worthy of diligent notes—but it was Saturday morning, I was bored, and he was the only dude talking to me at that moment.

HEY. GOOD TO SEE YOU TOO. RYAN, RIGHT?

WOW. GOOD MEMORY.

I grinned into the screen.

I'M PRETTY GOOD WITH NAMES, ESPECIALLY ONLINE.

I really wasn't.

I SEE THAT. SO...WHAT ARE YOU UP TO THESE DAYS?

WELL, I MOVED TO ATLANTA. GOT A NEW APART-MENT AND JOB. NOW I'M JUST TRYING TO FIGURE THIS PLACE OUT AND MAKE IT MY HOME. WHAT ABOUT YOU?

ATLANTA? REALLY? I LIVE IN ATLANTA.

Huh. Guess I never thought to ask that when we initially spoke. I'd just assumed he lived in Nashville.

REALLY? HOW COOL. WE'RE NEIGHBORS NOW.

WHERE IN TOWN DO YOU LIVE?

MIDTOWN. RIGHT IN THE MIDDLE OF THE GAY BUBBLE.

LOL, GAY BUBBLE IS RIGHT. I'M UP IN NORCROSS —OUTSIDE THE BELTWAY. MOST GUYS CONSIDER THAT ANOTHER COUNTRY.

There was a brief pause as I watched the cursor blink and tried to come up with something else witty. We'd talked a whole three minutes with no sexual references or requests for pictures. Something was different about this guy.

HEY. SORRY TO CHAT AND RUN, BUT I GOTTA GO. TALK TO YOU LATER?

SURE.

His name vanished from my friends list. He seemed nice enough, but didn't capture my attention enough to quash the chat-fever that consumed me. For the briefest moment, I wondered if my chatting was borne out of loneliness, horniness, or curiosity surrounding the men in my new community. I wasn't in the mood for a deep philosophical debate, so I chalked it up to all three and resumed the mission at hand (so to speak).

I spent another thirty minutes scrolling through the chat rooms, looking at profiles and introducing myself to the Atlanta boys. There were more ATLM4M rooms than I thought possible. If there were thirty-one flavors of bar in town, there were hundreds of subtle tastes online. I didn't know what half the acronyms meant, but the guys in the chat rooms understood their meaning on an intimate level and they weren't shy about saying so. Holy cow, these guys were forward—and some of them had interests that went beyond what my little devil might suggest. One guy sent me a picture of him underneath a glass-top table watching another guy drop his poop on the glass. I clicked LOG OFF as fast as I could and jumped back from my keyboard as if it was about to bite me—or poop on me.

I really didn't care that Mr. Poop-N-Peek got his jollies from something I found repulsive, but *yuck*. Poop watching? Really?

I did learn some useful information though. Besides AOL, a couple of newer websites now offered dating services similar to Match.com but for the gays. Two kept popping up in conversation, usually in the form of, "What's your name on Manhunt or Adam4Adam?" After the first time or two, I noticed a pattern. The guys who asked about Manhunt were definitely *on a hunt*, and not for pheasant or elk. They wanted the all-mighty ram, and they wanted it *now*. Those asking about A4A, as they abbreviated it, sounded more like traditional daters looking to get to know someone. I'm not saying the Manhunt guys weren't nice or ultimately hoping to meet someone for conversation, but, let's face it, they were on a site with the word "hunt" in it. We weren't exchanging recipes or inviting each other to the church social.

Curious, I opened my browser and went to the first site my lizard brain could handle: Manhunt.

Holy bejesus.

Half-naked men popped up. And by half naked, I mean *totally* naked with the naughty bits blurred out —and those naughty bits were going inside other dudes' naughty-bit holders. Bit grippers? Bit bums?

Asses. They were sticking their dicks in asses, okay?

The PK in me was shocked. The twentysomething, seriously repressed dude in me was elated.

The site made me register before I could go further, so I created a screen name that I thought described my interests. This was a dating site, wasn't it?

ATLSportsGuy. I liked sports and I lived in Atlanta. Seemed clear to me.

It, however, wasn't clear to some of the guys on Manhunt, who were into things I had yet to discover.

Have you ever heard of a golden shower? I hadn't. The second guy to message me asked if we could do that together. He wanted to do it all over my chest. He described, in great detail, how he wanted to lick it off and—

He wanted to pee on me. Really?

Unable to just walk away, I asked him why he thought I would be interested in his offer. He pointed to my screen name, thinking it was short for water sports, yet another reference to guys enjoying whizzing on each other. When I told him I meant softball and volleyball, he replied with the popular ROFL and called me a rookie.

I *was* a rookie—couldn't be mad at him for that.

I thanked him for his interest and moved on.

As I scrolled through the guys, I was again amazed by the variety and hotness of the men in Atlanta. Black, white, brown—and every color in between—and *so many* of them were ripped and sexy. Whatever flavor I wanted, it was there for the taking, and Manhunt made it easy. It was like all the NOW chat rooms on AOL bundled into one site, complete with an easy-to-use filter so a user could hunt in the most efficient way possible.

I chuckled at the idea of efficient sex. Was that even a thing? I guessed it was now.

The newness of the experience and the images of

the guys, some of which left absolutely nothing to the imagination, were getting me excited. Little Michael was rearing his head, tickled further by the silky shorts I was wearing, sans undies. The Manhunt dudes were advertising their best qualities, and damn, some of them had amazing, erect, perfectly curved qualities. Uncut qualities. Qualities with the barest leak of silky white—

Shit. I had to stop.

Desperate for a cold shower, I decided to check out Adam4Adam. As promised, it was almost a mirror of Match.com, with images of guys mostly clothed. Some held dogs or cats, others wore suits (that seemed a tad weird on a dating site). Profiles were filled with hobbies and interests, places they'd visited, even detailed descriptions of their ideal mate. After the testosterone-fueled heat of Manhunt, this was refreshing.

Don't get me wrong, I loved the sexy, gritty, let's-get-to-it quality of Manhunt. My heart was still racing from one brief visit to the site, but I knew I wanted more than a hookup long term. What I had with Carter, however brief our time had been, showed me that clearly. Rolling in the hay—or, in my case, having your hands tied above your head while a hot-as-fuck flight attendant banged me into the last decade—was insanely hot fun, but that was the *icing* on the cake. It wasn't *the cake*. Icing looked and tasted amazing, but it was fattening and bad for you and devoid of any lasting nutritional value.

Making cottage cheese with canned fruit together every night had substantive value. Tucking the boys in, kissing their tiny foreheads while they gripped my hand, that had true meaning. Doing the dishes shoulder to shoulder or sitting in a breakfast café without speaking—just being together—those were the moments that made a life together beautiful.

There was no way to replace the cake with the icing, no matter how many hot and horny hookups I enjoyed.

Thoroughly cooled down by my ruminations, I checked my new A4A inbox, expecting messages of introduction or pleasantries, maybe an invitation to coffee or dinner.

Come over and pound me was all Trevor4Love said.

Maybe the two sites weren't *that* different. We were guys, after all.

That was what Dwayne had warned me about before he left.

The thought of my old friend made me smile. I needed a dose of Dwayne, but it was still early in Nashville and he was a late riser most days. I vowed to call him later and catch up.

Another item on my checklist was looking into the high school basketball officiating associations in town. After ten years of work in Nashville, I'd built up some seniority among that group and dreaded breaking into a new one. Would they assign based on merit or would the group be a politicized, good ole boys' network? Would the basketball be any good? Would I have to drive a million miles in Atlanta's infamous traffic to work for pennies on the dollar? Oh, and what did officials get paid down here?

I had so many questions.

A quick search found there were four or five associations that serviced schools in the Metro Atlanta area. That boggled my mind. Our group in Nashville covered surrounding counties, and it was fairly common to drive outside the city to work. That one city needed four or five governing bodies made my head spin.

I clicked on the first group and found the president's name and number listed on the home page. Ten minutes later, I'd learned all about round ball in Atlanta. Mr. Prez said he would love to have some fresh blood in his group, but explained that their territory covered areas well outside the drive I'd wanted to make during a workweek. He then steered me clear of a couple groups known for shunning new folks, referring me to the group he thought best suited to my experience level and locale. It was spring, so there was plenty of time to meet the locals and work some AAU games for exposure and experience.

Atlanta had come through again—this time with my greatest passion, something unrelated to guys or bars or anything gay. I was sure someone would eventually revoke my gay card for that offense.

12

CARIBOU SEASON

The sun rose on a beautiful spring Sunday. Only a few wisps of cloud dotted the crystal-blue Atlanta sky. A light breeze tickled the hair on my arms. I'd learn in a few months how much every Atlantan misses that breeze when the town's stifling summer roasts everything in sight.

Curious about the softball league and what it would be like to participate in a gay sport with so many other guys, I drove across town to the fields where games were played. The first thing I noticed was the sheer number of fields in play at any given time. Back in Nashville, we generally had two or three games going at once. Here, there were eight fields filled with players, with several other teams watching from the sidelines, waiting for their game's start time.

And then there was the sheer number of guys.

If each field held two teams of a dozen or more, and there were eight fields occupied each hour, by my shoes-on math, that meant nearly two hundred dudes were actively competing every hour. I don't know which surprised me more: the number of gay guys gathered in one place, or my ability to sort through that math in my head.

The presence of uniforms surprised me. Each team was decked out in unique colors and logos; just like in straight leagues, but with one subtle difference. The gay teams' names were far cleverer and often carried either a snarky or sexual overtone. There were the Head Hunters, P-Cocks, the Dangling Darlings, I'd Hit That, the Morning Wood, the Packers, and, my personal favorite, Pitch Slapped. That last one had me giggling as I walked from one field to the next.

Even the league itself had a clever name: the Hotlanta Softball League.

Jokes aside, the boys took their games seriously. I half expected silliness and shenanigans, but even the lower-level players were intent on winning; well, except for a few teams who never stood much hope of winning—ever. It was easy to spot the purely social teams. Some of them wore colorful boas around their necks, or skirts instead of shorts. There was even a team of bears wearing tutus. Lord, help me. Every time one of them dropped a fly ball (which was *every* time one was hit to them), the entire team cried out, "OOPSIE!" and tossed their gloves into the air, giggling like embarrassed schoolgirls.

The athletic ability on that field was about as low as it could get, but the entertainment factor was off the chart. I watched several innings just to see how they reacted to different Bad News Bears level plays. If a particularly loud laugh or applause came from the crowd, several of the tutu-clad clan would turn and curtsey, then give several Miss America waves as though they'd won something special. They were hilarious—and they knew it.

After a thoroughly amusing morning of softball, I headed to the gym for my daily workout, then hit Cowtippers for my usual grilled chicken and baked sweet potato. I'd eaten there so often that the waiters (no waitresses—this was Midtown, after all) didn't even ask what I wanted. My tall glass of iced water waited on the table before I was seated, and food arrived faster than McDonald's could toss a toy into a Happy Meal box. It was tasty, healthy, and super-fast—and the eye candy was fabulous, especially on a weekend when the patio was filled with boys.

I got home around three o'clock and decided to quash my boredom with another round of AOL chatting. The warm tones of Mr. AOL greeted me with the ever-familiar, "You've got mail." Those were always welcome words. I'm sure there was a scientific explanation, some endorphin release or such. All I know is it made me giddy thinking someone had sent me a note.

Hey, again!

I was still skimming the Crate and Barrel coupon email when an IM popped up. It was RAL2027. Two days in a row? We'd gone a couple years between conversations, then months, and now he was chatting on back-to-back days? Interesting.

Hey, Ryan. Whatcha up to?

Nothing, really. Bored. Goofing off. U?

Nada. Just worked out and ate.

We'd chatted for an hour before I realized how much time had passed. Losing an hour like that wasn't unusual when I had five or six chat windows going at once, but to spend an hour talking to only one guy was…unexpected.

Ryan read my mind.

We've been chatting for over an hour and you haven't made one sexual reference.

Is that allowed on here? Ha ha.

Are you asking me to talk dirty to you? I was proud of that twist.

That wasn't exactly what I meant, but feel free. I'm a big boy.

Oh, really? How big?

OMG, NOW I'M BLUSHING.

I'd really enjoyed our conversation to this point, but the sheer cuteness of his response made me grin.

Then I thought about our past chats. We'd never once talked about anything sexual. He was right. That *was* out of the norm. I liked to get naughty as much as the next guy, but in that moment, the fact we hadn't even mentioned sex struck me as really cool.

I'll never be sure if it was my tiny angel or devil guiding me, but I decided to ask Ryan to meet. As I started to type, I heard a ding.

WE SHOULD MEET—FOR REAL.

Holy shit. He'd beaten me to the punch.

I wasn't intimidated by the idea of meeting in person. I'd met plenty of guys from online, either for coffee or dinner, or just to hook up—okay, *mostly* to hook up. What can I say? Let a preacher's kid off his leash and watch out. I had years of repressed time to make up for.

"Darn right. *Repressed* doesn't even begin to describe what you were." My leather-clad demon appeared with a dramatic puff on my shoulder. For some reason, his tiny vest was splayed open and his chest looked oiled. Is an imaginary conscience supposed to lube himself up before offering guidance?

Why was I nervous about meeting this Ryan guy? Technically, we'd been chatting online for years, though we'd actually lost touch throughout most of that time. Still, it felt like we'd been chatting for a long time. His conversations were comfortable and easy, and if his stats were accurate, he was a tasty morsel. It seemed so silly for me to get the jitters now. I laughed at my own silliness and sucked in a breath before pecking at the keys again.

WE'VE BEEN CHATTING A WHILE ON HERE. SURE. WOULD BE NICE TO MEET.

NOW?

UH, SURE. WHERE?

YOU KNOW THE CARIBOU COFFEE IN MIDTOWN?

I remembered passing it dozens of times as I wandered around town, but would still need to look up directions. I didn't want him to know I was a complete idiot when it came to getting around.

YOU BET. SEE YOU IN TEN?

PERFECT. I'LL BE THE GUY IN THE BLUE SHIRT.

AWESOME. SEE YOU SOON.

I GOT TO THE COFFEE SHOP FIRST. UNSURE WHAT TO do, I grabbed a booth and waited for a dude in a blue shirt with blond hair who was about my height. That wasn't exactly a Columbo-level description, but it would have to do. My fingers wouldn't stop fiddling with each other. The place was busy, and customers entered and exited in a blur of caffeine-induced perpetual motion. Every time the little bell attached to the door tinkled, my head snapped up, hoping to get a first glance.

Then I realized I'd broken the most sacred law of online dating.

Always, always, *always* get a picture—or several —in different settings, if possible, using different angles, and with a newspaper to verify the date and authenticity.

Yes, I was a bit of an online dating freak.

I'd done *none* of that with Ryan.

I had no idea what he really looked like and was sitting there anxiously awaiting his grand entrance. For all I knew, he could be eighty, bald, and have three horns poking out of his head. Alright, he wouldn't have the horns, but you get my drift. I knew nothing—and any self-respecting gay knows his first job *is* to judge the book by its cover. How could I do that when I hadn't ever seen the book? Ryan's profile was woefully bereft of stars, much less the special circled kind, because I'd been derelict in my AOL trolling duties.

My nervousness grew as I pondered how careless I'd been.

"Three creams and one Splenda, right?"

I jolted out of my seat, banging my knees on the bottom of the table and knocking myself back onto the booth. When I looked up, my blond blind date had an amused grin on his face and a cup of coffee in each hand. He set the cups down.

"Hi, I'm Ryan."

Yes, you are, I thought.

His online description, though sparse, had been accurate. It had, however, left out the crystal blue-gray eyes that twinkled down at me. Paired with his blond hair and broad smile, they were dreamy, almost wolf-like. I thought he was handsome; Normal Hot, not Hollywood Hot. Cover models might make great pin-ups, but Ryan's ordinary good looks were endearing, somehow more real than so much of the perfection I'd seen walking around Atlanta.

His profile had specified 16a, meaning his arms were sixteen inches when measured with tape—but that stat never sank in. I needed a visual—and his biceps gave me more than an eyeful. Sixteen inches never looked so good.

Now, stop that. Sixteen inches *down there* is unreasonable—unless you're Catherine the Great's horse.

"Uh, hey. I'm Michael. How'd you know how I like my coffee?"

Yes, that was the first thing I said to him. I am a total moron.

He shrugged and dropped into the chair across from me. "You mentioned it a while back, maybe a year ago."

Holy crap. How did he remember a detail like that from an online conversation we had a year ago? Did he have a secret notebook too?

"Do I look okay?" he asked.

I'd finally gotten over the knee-bumping incident enough to return to my smart-ass self. I scanned him up and down with an exaggerated gaze.

"Yeah, I suppose you'll do—for coffee."

He chuckled and raised his cup in salute, then took a drink. "Not bad yourself."

I blushed and ducked my head. "Thanks."

We'd arrived around four thirty in the afternoon. When the clock chimed seven times, Ryan glanced at his watch and let out a long sigh.

"I can't believe we've been here this long. I need to get home. Tomorrow's a school day."

We walked to the parking lot together and leaned awkwardly against one of the building's pillars, staring at each other.

"I can't remember the last time I talked to someone for so long and didn't want to escape halfway through." He smiled sheepishly and tiny divots appeared. The man had dimples to go with the sparkling eyes. I fought back a swoon.

"Yeah, I had a great time," I said.

"Okay, I really gotta go. See you online later?"

I nodded. He leaned forward, then pulled back, then stretched out a hand and patted my arm. Yeah, it was totally awkward, but in a weird way it was perfectly suited to our coffee date.

13

HI, BARRIER!

The next day, Connie bounded into my office, her endless energy and infectious smile overpowering my non-morning-person desire to smack the life out of her cheery disposition.

"We need to do a sales contest. My team is bored with the comp plan, and I think we can use something like this to make people *like* working here for a change."

"Okay. What did you have in mind?"

She plopped into a chair and scooted it forward so she could rest her elbows on my desk. "I have no idea. We need to brainstorm, but I have a team meeting in five minutes, and the afternoon is back-to-back."

"I guess we could get together after work. Today is my off-gym day."

"Perfect. It's a date." She winked and hopped up

from her chair. "You can drag me to one of those gay bars you told me about last week."

And with that crazy seed planted, she vanished.

At five thirty, she reappeared in my doorway. "Stop working. We have brainstorming and gay gawking to do!"

I couldn't decide if her enthusiasm for this little adventure amused or scared me. Connie and I had been to lunch countless times over the month or so we'd been working together. She'd become my closest friend and confidant, but taking her to a gay bar was uncharted territory. Hell, other than Dwayne, I'd never taken anyone else—unless you counted the boys I had escorted *out* of the bars.

No, they didn't count.

It felt like I was about to expose a part of my life I'd kept carefully segregated from every other part. It sounds silly now, but at the time, that thought was terrifying. Would she still see me the same way after an hour with me in the gays' natural habitat? Would she still respect me? Would our working relationship change? Would our friendship?

Poof. "You're overthinking and not giving *her* enough credit. Go, have fun. Drool over the boys. Maybe have a drink—something *other* than a Coke for a change." The devil had changed out of his leather and donned a sharp blue suit with a crisp white shirt and tastefully patterned tie. His raven hair was slicked back and somehow his eyes sparkled the color of emeralds.

Damn, even my devil was starting to look hot to me. I really needed therapy.

Not to be outdone, the angel appeared. He now wore a Catholic priest-like robe, but in white, like the Pope. "For once, I agree with Sparky over there—except for the part about what you drink. Coca-Cola is perfectly respectable and pleasantly fizzy. Stay on the path, Michael."

Was that encouragement or a lesson?

With another poof, they vanished, and I realized Connie was still standing in my doorway watching me. One brow was raised, her lips were turned up in an odd quirk, and her arms were crossed beneath her ample boobs, both of which were staring at me with their one good eye through her white shirt.

"Alright," I said, stuffing a folder into my desk drawer and locking it. "Let's do this."

CONNIE AND I GIGGLED ACROSS THE TABLE AT Cowtippers, tossing out one crazy idea after another. Some were actually serious and went on her list, scrawled in meticulous handwriting that made my illegible scribble look more like the ramblings of a third grader than a professional adult. I watched her write a long description and smiled as I realized how close we'd become in such a short time. She was the kindest, most positive person I'd met in years. She smiled easily and brought laughter into every room she entered. You could *feel* her walk into a room. It was a special gift I'd only known a few to possess. On top of all that, she made me laugh so much my side hurt—and no topic was safe from her sharp wit.

I switched into full salesman mode. "We need to do something big. Ted thinks waving a stack of Benjamins around will get the team fired up, but that only works on a few of them. We've got to capture their imagination as much as their competitive spirit."

She thought a moment, then came a twinkle in her eyes that told me something amazing was about to come out of her mouth. "What's more magical than a trip to Paris?"

"Okay, I'm listening."

"Think about it. The Eiffel Tower, the Arc de Triomphe, the Louvre—even simple scenes of people eating at outdoor cafés while tourists stroll by. Everything about Paris screams sexy and exciting. We can decorate the whole office in French flags and banners."

She propped her body up and tucked her legs under her butt, then leaned forward on the table and giggled. Thirty minutes later, we had a fully baked plan to present to Ted, complete with a budget, decoration layout for the office, and a sketch of flyers we would create detailing the rules. She let her legs drop and settled her butt back onto the booth, excitement ebbing as I paid for dinner.

"Okay, that's done. Where are you taking me now?" she asked in the eager voice of a teenage girl who was out past curfew.

I chuckled. "It's Monday at seven o'clock. The only place with any crowd will be Blake's."

"Look at you, already knowing which bar is busy when."

"Yeah. It's part of a new gay's compulsory training."

She laughed and levered herself out of the booth. "Awesome. Let's go, my knight in rainbow armor."

Arm in arm, we laughed our way to the car, then drove the few blocks to Atlanta's most famous stand-and-model bar. It was exactly as I'd expected: sparsely filled with a handful of gaggles clustered in twos and threes, either at the bar or around high-top tables scooched against walls. Connie grabbed a table while I flirted with the bartender and ordered drinks. I returned a moment later and presented her with a Sex on the Beach, then set my Coke down in front of my stool.

"Oh no you don't. Go back up to that hottie behind the bar and get a real drink. It's rude to make a lady drink alone." I followed the line of her index finger to find the grinning bartender. He gave me a wave.

"Fine. You win. Be right back."

When I returned, Jack had joined my Coke. Then the interrogation began.

"So, how did coffee go with Ryan?"

She never forgot *anything*.

We'd had to complete a form a few weeks back that required my social security number. She had written it *one* time and could still recite it. That was impressive *and* scary. I shouldn't have been surprised she remembered the random online coffee date's name.

"It was fine."

She cocked her head as she sipped her drink, then giggled at how strong it was.

"Fine? That's all I get? I ask you to take me to Paris and you drive me to Decatur?"

"Hey! Decatur has charm. Have you been downtown?"

She rolled her eyes. "Go on. Out with it. I want details."

There was no escaping her steely glare. "He's

nice. I hadn't seen a pic before we met, so I really didn't know what to expect. He works out a lot—I could see that in his arms and how his chest filled out his shirt. He's blond. That's new for me. I usually like guys with dark hair, more Italian or Latino—but he's handsome. He has weird lips. The bottom one kind of pooches out." I made an attempt at mimicking Ryan's lower lip, and she cackled.

"What did you talk about?"

"Oh, wow. A lot. We talked for a few hours."

Her right brow shot up. "A few hours? For coffee?"

I nodded.

"That's a lot of talking for a first date."

"Yeah, it was—and it was easy. You know how sometimes it's a struggle to keep a conversation going with someone new, to think of something to say to fill the awkward spaces? There wasn't a single moment of dead space to fill. It felt good. He seems like a really nice guy."

She threw back the last of her drink, and I knew I was in trouble. She was getting tipsy.

"When are you seeing him again?"

"I don't know." I shrugged. "He's nice and all, but I wasn't blown away—and I'm still fresh meat, as Dwayne would say. I can't tie myself down before I see what else might be on the menu." I raised my cup.

"Plus, there's something odd I can't put my finger on with him. We'll talk for hours on AOL, several days in a row, then he'll disappear for a week. Before I moved here, he vanished for over a year. By the time he resurfaced, I'd forgotten who he was."

"Everyone doesn't live on that dumb computer. You could get out and meet people in person."

"I am. I go out almost every Friday and Saturday night—haven't missed *meeting* a guy yet." I winked and stood to get us another round. "Something feels weird with Ryan, though. I don't know. Maybe *I'm* being weird."

She laughed. "That's *definitely* not a first."

We had two more rounds. Connie switched to water with lime for her third drink, but insisted I needed to keep going with the stronger stuff. She was enjoying the insanity that tumbled out of my mouth when I was well lubricated. Midway through that third drink, the lights in the bar dimmed and loud music boomed. A drag queen standing over six feet tall, wearing high heels and a headdress that added another couple feet of height, sauntered into the room with a microphone in her hand. Guys streamed in from every entrance until they were crammed shoulder to shoulder. An irreverent monologue of jokes and jibes was followed by familiar, upbeat songs that had every gay in the place singing along and waving their hands in the air.

Connie laughed the entire time. I thought she was going to hyperventilate—or piddle. My alcohol-induced giggle wasn't much better and fed off her perpetual, childlike laughter. We were a complete mess and loving every minute of it.

After the show, she drove my car back to Cowtippers. She cackled every time my head swiveled and I pointed out the next hot guy walking down the street.

"You're gonna hurt your neck one of these days," she quipped.

"Ooh, look at that one!" I pointed excitedly at a dude jogging shirtless. His chiseled chest bounced with every stride. I made a *boingy-boingy* sound in time with his footfalls. "Daaaaaaamn."

She playfully slapped my arm. "I swear you'd think a road sign was hot."

On cue, we passed a construction crew erecting wooden horses to block pedestrian traffic on the sidewalk. I snapped my head dramatically and said, "Hi, barrier!"

She snorted, and we both fell into another tear-filled fit.

14

PUTT-PUTT IS REAL GOLF

Ted approved our proposal the next day, and we scheduled a rollout meeting for the sales and recruiting staff on Thursday. Connie could barely contain herself. We hit every party store we could find, grabbing everything in the iconic blue, white and red. By the time Thursday arrived, every desk had a miniature French flag, there was bunting draped throughout the office, and French music greeted employees as they entered our suite. I have to give her credit; Connie's enthusiasm was even more infectious than her laugh. The troops were pumped before the meeting even began, and exploded in applause and cheers as she revealed the grand prize.

Connie and I were already well liked by our teams. Ted ruled with an iron fist and didn't understand how to motivate people. Connie and I genuinely cared about them, and that made all the difference. Throw in a chance to go to Paris, and we became instant rock stars.

Each day of the contest, we passed out a different French-themed goodie. One day it was cookies, the next croissants, then buttons with French colors. It generated so much buzz that groups would gather in the mornings to await whatever the day's surprise would be. Connie insisted we sing our surprise one morning. I'm pretty sure the troops wanted their money back from that concert.

We also crafted daily prizes so everyone could win something, even if they fell behind in the main horse race. Those contests became the backbone of growth for our sales campaign, with the bulk of my salespeople clearly out of the hunt for Paris.

In a matter of weeks, the monotonous rhythm that pervaded the office had been replaced by playful French accents and shouts of "Oh là là" when someone made a sale. It was silly and crazy, but brilliant. Connie was a miracle worker, and we were great partners.

We were so busy that first week that I hardly thought about Ryan. I barely even logged on to AOL.

Friday, after a painful workout, I flopped into my wobbly office chair and powered up my PC. AOL's normally friendly voice seemed annoyed at the volume of emails stacked up in my queue, growling "You've got mail" as the hourglass flipped.

Deep in the pile were two emails from Ryan.

TUESDAY 9:47 P.M.

HEY. JUST WANTED TO SAY I REALLY ENJOYED COFFEE. HOPE YOU'RE HAVING A GOOD WEEK.

RYAN

I MOVED DOWN THE LIST AND OPENED THE SECOND.

WEDNESDAY 9:29 P.M.

HEY AGAIN. JUST REALIZED I NEVER SENT YOU A PIC. ENJOY.

R

THE EMAILS WERE INNOCUOUS ENOUGH, AND I WAS flattered he'd thought about me. It was more than I could say. I liked him fine, but just didn't feel that burning passion after we'd met. Maybe that was a good thing. Maybe we're supposed to be a little less *enthused* and more intellectually intrigued. I don't know. After my introduction to gay intimacy by Fly

Boy and his silk ties, I knew I wanted passion, but I also wanted to be challenged with good conversation.

Was it too much to ask for both?

"Yes, moron. Just let Little Michael drive the car, and we'll all be fine." The devil appeared, in fishnet stockings and a pink leotard. That was new. How could I take his counsel seriously when he dressed like that?

"You're growing, Michael. I'm proud of you." The angel's soothing voice flowed into my other ear. He materialized on my shoulder in a shimmering white three-piece suit with a golden tie. He looked like he was ready to host a game show, but maybe that's what heaven really was—one big, cosmic game show.

I shook my head free of the lace and glitter. "Guys, I'm not really interested in Ryan, okay?"

The devil huffed something inaudible, then vanished. The angel actually laughed as he winked out. Weird.

I clicked the little paperclip, and a headshot of Ryan filled the screen. It looked like his work ID picture. He was handsome enough, even if his lower lip pooched out oddly. I stared at it for a second, rotating the pic ninety degrees to see if it changed. Nope. It was still poochy. For a successful dude, he really didn't have any online dating game. Who sends a stiff, fully clothed pic that doesn't extend below the shoulders? I closed his pic and moved on.

When the rest of my overstuffed inbox proved as disappointing as Ryan's pic, I decided it was time to see what other fish the Atlanta sea might have to offer. I pulled up the list of rooms, beginning with Atlanta-M4M, and searched for one I hadn't entered before.

Ding.

HEY. YOU'RE BACK.

He had a quick trigger finger—and his IM let me know he'd added me to *his* friends list too. That made me smile. Who doesn't love a little flattery?

HEY, YOURSELF. HOW WAS YOUR WEEK?

GOOD. BUSY AT THE OFFICE. I WORKED UNTIL 8 OR SO MOST DAYS.

OUCH, I said. THAT SOUNDS PAINFUL.

I'M USED TO IT. WE HAVE PEOPLE OVERSEAS, SO I HAVE TO DO CALLS DURING THEIR WORKDAY HOURS. IT MAKES FOR A LATE NIGHT.

I scrolled through chat rooms, not really paying attention to our conversation.

I HAVE AN IDEA.

When he didn't elaborate, I typed, OKAY, FIRE AWAY.

WHEN'S THE LAST TIME YOU PLAYED PUTT-PUTT?

Well, that was random. I clicked the chat rooms closed. Now he had my attention.

Umm, I don't remember. Years. Maybe since I was a kid.

You're still a kid.

Ha ha. Smart ass, Grandpa. How old are you anyway? You never told me.

That's me, a smart ass;) So, putt-putt with me tomorrow?

When I didn't answer right away, he added, I have to warn you. I used to play semi-pro golf. You won't win, but it should be fun watching you try.

That little bitch.

Oh, it's on now. Bring your clubs or whatever you need, old man. You're going down.

I was hoping you'd say that eventually.

Ha. I'm talking putt-putt.

Yeah, right. Just don't get your hopes up. You're still going to lose.

We agreed on a time and place, then he logged off, claiming he had another work call or something—on a Friday night. Something still felt weird, but I loved a challenge, and his playful banter was on point. I had to admit, Ryan made me smile.

"Told ya," my white-suited friend said as he puffed into existence, hands planted firmly on his hips in the teapot pose. "Keep an open mind. I have a good feeling about this one."

The devil, back in his black biker leathers, leaned in front of my chin and stuck his tongue out at the angel. "Just get some dick and move on. You're too young to get tied down—unless you're getting *tied up*."

Those two really needed therapy.

THE NEXT MORNING, AFTER A TUMBLER OF COFFEE and two packets of cherry frosted Pop-Tarts, I tossed on my Nashville Rocks T-shirt and a pair of khaki shorts and headed to the course—okay, the putt-putt place. I'd never been on a real golf course, but I was pretending this was the Masters, complete with a green jacket waiting for me after I nailed the clown face on the last hole.

I didn't have any expectations built up for the date. My recollection of Ryan was of a nice, handsome-enough guy who held down a good conversation. I hadn't been particularly smitten, and looked at the day as a fun time with a friend more than a date. The thrill of competition against a cocky opponent was more rooted in my mind than, well, his root—or anything else about him.

I pictured the end-of-day scene in my mind:

Park attendants wearing green polo shirts were

lined up and clapping, while the nerdy, bespectacled manager helped me put the winner's jacket on for the first time. Thousands of fans lined the green—okay, tens and tens of people lined the game room—all smiling and applauding, amazed at my unparalleled golfing prowess. They'd even play 'Eye of the Tiger' in the background. Nothing said crushing victory like a *Rocky* theme. Ryan was standing off to the side, a mix of jealousy and disappointment on his face as his embarrassing defeat sank in.

It was a beautiful scene. I might've even shed a tear at the end.

Who needed therapy now?

I pulled into the parking lot, surprised to find it nearly empty on a Saturday. So much for my poetic scene with the dozens of applauding fans. I parked beside Ryan's silver Honda and walked through the main gate to the hut where guests purchased tickets for golf or go-karts. Ryan was standing a few feet from the hut. He waved, and I nearly tripped over a curb.

When we'd first met at Caribou, Ryan wore sensible, business casual clothing; a polo shirt and khaki pants. I don't know what I expected that day at putt-putt, but it wasn't a neon yellow tank top—you know, the kind the muscle heads at the gym wear with the stringy shoulder straps and deeply cut sides? The wind was blowing lightly, billowing his shirt so I could see his perfectly cut abs and protruding chest through the sides. He smiled, beaming perfect pearly whites at me. His blond hair, something I'd never found terribly attractive, blew in the wind—yes, like Marilyn's dress —and I swear the sun behind him cast a glow.

In that sun-blind moment, I knew I was in trouble. My heart raced, and I immediately worried English would be my second language if I tried to speak. What was happening? I wasn't even that interested in this guy.

I looked up and *holy shit*, he was beautiful. No, he was stunning. Striking? Fucking hot.

Where had *that* come from? My brain, heart, and Little Michael—all of them—were rebelling and going in a direction I hadn't anticipated. Today was about crushing the opposition, not ogling him.

"Hey, you okay?"

Ryan gripped my arm to help me from my near-tumble. His skin against mine sent a wave of fire up my arm and into my already turbulent chest. I glanced up and our eyes met.

"Yeah, I, uh, thanks. I tripped. I'm good."

He smiled and kept his hand on my arm as we walked to the hut—long after I'd righted myself and no longer needed help. I reveled in his touch, in his hand staying connected. My mind spun.

"Grab your balls," Ryan said, pulling me out of my—whatever that was.

"What? My—"

He rolled his eyes and chuckled, then grabbed a club and pretended to swing it, measuring the balance or something. I watched the way he gripped and swung with practiced ease and knew my dream of a green jacket was in as much jeopardy as any thought of not being attracted to Mr. Sexy Chest. I grabbed the first club I saw and a blue ball.

He started laughing.

"What?"

"I'm not sure which is funnier, you picking the kids' club or declaring your blue balls in public."

I looked down. The club was short. No, it was *tiny*, sized for a child of six or so. Then I glanced at the ball in my hand and caught on to his joke.

"Just don't want you feeling overconfident," I said, then quickly replaced the club with an adult version. On a whim, I grabbed a black ball and held it up for him. He raised a brow. "It's symbolic of the death of your pride, Mr. Semi-Pro."

He barked a laugh. "We'll see about that. You don't know what you've signed up for today."

He had no idea how true that was.

ON TWO OUT OF THE FIRST THREE HOLES, RYAN putted a hole-in-one. If he hadn't been so cute, the smug smirk twisting his poochy lip might've been annoying. He clearly knew his way around a golf club, and I was beginning to think all my smack talk was going to bite me in the butt—and not in the fun way.

By the midpoint, which Ryan proclaimed "the turn," he was ahead by more than ten strokes.

"You can concede at any point. I won't think less of you."

I rolled my eyes dramatically and pointed my club at him. "I'm about to get a very different ball in with this club, mister. Your turn."

He snickered. "Testy, testy."

"Testy-cle is what you risk by not taking your turn."

He laughed, eyeing me for a moment before turning to line up his next shot. Hole ten was based on blind luck. There were two tunnels on the side of a faux mountain. One dribbled down to a very likely hole-in-one. The other took the ball into a hellscape of obstacles, including a water trap that was clearly marked "three-stroke penalty" in creepy Halloween font. The real twist in this guessing game was that the paths through the mountain were hidden. There was no way to walk the course and see which hole led where.

I see you snickering. Get your mind out of the gutter!

Like the unfortunate dude in *Indiana Jones and the Temple of Doom,* Mr. God-Given Golfer chose poorly. He stroked his putt and the ball *swooshed* through the right-side hole without hitting the sides. We ran around the mountain, giggling like five-year-olds, then waited impatiently as the ball rattled around and plopped out into the desert of doom, bouncing off several obstacles, then creeping its way to the edge of the water hazard. Ryan bent over and pretended to blow on it, desperate to keep it dry. I called foul at his antics and hopped with glee as the ball finally splashed into the water.

"Plus three! I need the judge to mark that down." I did a happy dance to rub it in.

He play-shoved me. "You're still *way* behind, young man. Go take your turn."

"Yes, Dad."

His shove became a tad less playful at that.

"Now, now. No abusing your far younger companion."

I hopped away before the next shove could land.

Going second on that hole was a huge advantage. I tapped my ball down the left-side path and danced a jig as it fell out of the mountain and rolled directly into the cup.

"One!"

He gave me a mini-clap, tapping his fingertips primly against his other palm like an aristocratic lady. "Bravo. About time you got one."

"Oh, I'm just warming up. All those other holes were just to make you feel good."

And another shove, this time with a squeeze of my bicep. I looked up from his hand to find him smiling appreciatively. I couldn't think of a single smart-ass thing to say.

"Alright, let me show you how to get out of a mess." He turned to retrieve his ball from the drink.

Five strokes—and one more trip to the pond later —the overall tally was dead even.

"I believe we now have a race, good sir." I smirked and squeezed his bicep like he'd done mine. It didn't budge.

Damn. Like, really. *Damn.*

"Don't hurt your hand," he said with a grin.

Again, my brain and mouth failed to communicate. I stammered something unintelligible and released his arm—reluctantly.

By the time we reached the final hole, Ryan was no longer laughing and shoving. He was all game face. I was giddy just to still be in it. We had traded holes-in-one following the mountain, leaving the score tied going into the dreaded clown face. Despite my big talk, I'd fully expected Ryan to wipe me off the course—but I actually had a shot at winning. He'd *never* live that down.

He squatted down and raised his club, taking in the lay of the land.

"This is mini-golf, not the Masters," I chirped from the side.

"Hush. I'm working over here." His head never turned, but I could see a hint of a smile crack his serious composure.

After the longest non-caddie-assisted pre-putt in the history of golf, his club struck. The ball rolled perfectly down the center of the turf, expertly missing the windmill's sails, and directly into the clown's gaping jaw.

"Hole-in-one! Top that," Ryan hooted, club raised in salute to the crowd that hadn't gathered.

I ignored the obvious sexually laced quip dying to fly off my tongue, and tried to act confident as I strode up to the tee. He brushed his shoulder against mine as he moved to watch. A hint of sweet cologne added a heady sensation to the thrill of his touch. I fought back a swoon and focused on the spinning windmill.

Just to be a smart ass, I squatted down and mimicked his lay-of-the-land thing, having no idea what I was looking for. He grunted—or laughed—I couldn't tell. I straightened, took a slow draw, and struck. He raced up beside me and watched as my ball followed the same perfect line his had traversed moments before—then smacked into one of the windmill's sails and bounced to the side. It dribbled back up the green to stop a foot in front of us.

Stupid traitor ball.

My head dropped dramatically, and Ryan rubbed my shoulder in consolation.

"There, there. You put up a great fight."

"Down to the last hole." I grinned up. "Bet you didn't think it would be that close."

He shook his head. "I really didn't."

We walked around the evil clown and his dastardly windmill to the hut to return our clubs. The sun was shining brightly above in a crystal-clear sky. We squinted in the glare.

"So…" he started.

We walked away from the hut toward the parking lot. I waited to see if he'd continue.

"That was a lot of fun."

"Yeah, it was," I agreed.

He stopped walking. "Want to grab lunch? I think there's a restaurant inside."

"Sure. Who knew golf could make ya work up such an appetite?"

"It's an athletic sport," he said.

I rolled my eyes and grinned. "Right, especially with clowns and windmills."

"Just 'cause you came in second—"

"Lord, you're going to remind me of that for years, aren't you?"

"If you're lucky." He grinned.

My head snapped up. I didn't think he meant what came out. He was just bantering and teasing—but he'd said it. His eyes told me he knew what he'd said, and he wasn't apologizing for it.

Unable to think, I said the only thing that came to mind. "Lunch?"

15

POOL PARTY

We wandered inside the entertainment complex's entrance, greeted by the bings and bongs of the video arcade at the far end of the massive room. A left turn led us into a restaurant decorated like a 1950s café, complete with slick, faux-leather booths framed in highly polished silver. Bouncy music played over crackly speakers.

The lights were dimmed, except for one tiny section of four tables brightly lit by neon wall decorations. The only sign of life in the place was a lone server bent over a dog-eared book at the counter. She didn't notice us walk in, and Ryan had to stand in front of her to get her attention, a move that startled the poor woman. His shoulders shivered with laughter as she nearly jumped out of her pink apron. Her book flew across the floor, and I grinned when Ryan knelt to retrieve it—both because of the way his lats and triceps flexed in his skimpy tank, and at his simple act of chivalry.

Chicken sandwiches and fries appeared to be the safest things on the menu, and despite being the only customers, they took a painfully long time to arrive. We barely noticed. Conversation flowed as if we'd known each other for a lifetime. One story led to a memory or snarky jibe, then streamed directly into some other tale or question or thought. Being with Ryan was easy and felt…good.

Did that even make sense on a second date? Was I *completely* insane?

"Yes, you are," the angel said on my shoulder, this time dressed in a white polo shirt with white-and-tan checkered golf pants popular in the 1930s. "But falling in love *is* insane, Michael. It's beautifully insane, and you'll never make sense of it. Just enjoy the moment, and follow your heart."

I was shocked to hear encouragement from the one usually yanking hard on my leash.

Then the devil appeared on the other shoulder dressed in tight, shiny faux leather and high heels. His whip cracked against my neck.

"Hey!"

He grinned. "Shut up and listen. For once, that angelic windbag has a point—but there's more to this dude than hot tits and arms. Something feels *off*, and I like that. Let's get him naked."

"Easy," the angel said, poking me with a tiny golf club I hadn't seen. "Take your time. If he's right, he'll be right tomorrow. Just enjoy the ride."

"Ha. He said 'ride.' That's *exactly* what I want you to do."

I shook my head clear, and the annoying little trolls vanished. When I looked up, Ryan was staring at me with a bemused set to his poochy lip.

"Penny," he said.

"Huh?"

"For your thoughts. I lost you there for a second. First time today."

My lips curled upward at that.

"Sorry, the voices in my head get into arguments sometimes, and I have to break them up."

He laughed at what he assumed was a joke. Somewhere in the back of my head, I heard the devil laughing too.

Ryan reached across the table. A bolt of lightning streaked from my fingers to my soul at his touch—his first real touch. He took my hand in both of his.

"I like your voices, Michael Reed. All of them." His crystal eyes stared into me, and I felt the café tilt.

What did one even say to that?

I smiled weakly and looked down at our hands. "Thanks. Me too. I mean, I don't like my own voice, or voices. Well, I do. They're funny sometimes, but that's not what I meant. I like your voice. That's what I meant."

His lips parted wide, and his eyes smiled even wider, if that was even a thing. I couldn't tell if he was more amused at my stammering or pleased that we seemed to be on the same page. I hoped it was the latter.

He sat back, stealing his hands from mine. It felt like the world had been pulled from my grasp.

The server arrived, and Ryan insisted on paying for lunch. It was about two o'clock now, and I figured this would be when we said our goodbyes.

I wasn't ready for goodbye.

"You like pool?" he asked with mischief in his voice.

I cocked my head. "Uh, sure. I guess."

He pointed across the café. "There's a table over there. I'm pretty good, but who knows? You might get lucky. Want to try for a little post-golf revenge?"

He wasn't saying goodbye.

I felt like a ten-year-old walking into a toy store. It was awesome.

"Bring it. I owe you *and* that clown."

He laughed. "Oh, so now I'm colluding with the clown? Is that how it went?"

"The clown, the kid with the clubs, pretty much everyone over there was on your side. I was lucky to keep things close. Now you're on your own, bucko. Just you, me, and the balls."

He barked another laugh as I turned four shades of red.

"The *pool* balls, dirty man."

"Don't forget my massively long cue. You can chalk the tip if you want."

I missed a step, and the crimson deepened. What the hell? I'd been tied to a bedpost without blushing. Why were this guy's terrible innuendos turning me into a bumbling schoolboy? Every time I blushed, it *encouraged* him, like a vampire smelling blood.

Over the course of five games of eight-ball, the sexual references flew faster than the cue ball. I'm pretty sure I laughed—and blushed—the whole time.

But I won.

"That's three out of five, good sir. Do you concede defeat or shall we continue?" I bowed dramatically like some vassal greeting his lord.

He racked his stick and glanced at his watch. "Wow."

"What?"

"It's five o'clock. We've been here almost since this place opened. I probably should head home."

There was an odd hint in his voice, the same one I'd picked up in his instant messages. He wasn't saying *something*—and it felt important.

"Got a hot date later?" I prodded playfully.

He grinned and shook his head. "No, just some work to do around the house."

We racked the balls and walked past the cacophony of sounds blaring from the arcade out into the fresh air of the parking lot. When we reached our cars, Ryan leaned against his and shoved his hands halfway into his pockets.

One perfectly pink nipple peeked out of his tank top. I couldn't stop staring at it.

He glanced down, and realization dawned. With a smirk, he pulled his tank top back just enough to show half his ridiculously rounded pec.

I still couldn't look away. *Damn.*

His smirk turned into a chuckle. "This was one of my best dates ever," he blurted out.

I finally tore my eyes away—reluctantly. "Mine too. I had a blast."

"Even in defeat?"

"Hey, I won pool. That's far more challenging than some fake golf game."

He laughed. "We can take our golf onto a real course, if putt-putt wasn't to your liking."

I shook my head. "Nah. I'm good. I might make a good bag kid for you, but that's about it."

"Bag kid? You mean caddie?"

"Oh yeah, caddie. Right." *Idiot.* I blushed again.

He reached out and brushed my arm lightly with his fingers. My skin pimpled, and I shivered.

"I'd like to see you again. Is that okay?"

"I'd really like that too."

"I would kiss you, but we're in a public parking lot." He looked around meaningfully.

For you liberated gays who enjoy holding hands and kissing in public, that wasn't always an option. One might find himself on the receiving end of an egg, or worse, a baseball bat; at the very least, some harsh words. Even Ryan reaching across the table and taking my hand would've raised more than a few eyebrows in most parts of town. We were lucky our bored server sported a rainbow tattoo on the inside of her wrist and barely gave us a second glance.

Our eyes held each other for a long moment. It felt like an embrace, the intimacy of that gaze.

"Alright. See you online later?" he asked.

"Sure. Drive safe," I said as he climbed into his car.

His door slammed shut, then his window rolled

down. "Worried about me already?" he asked with a poochy smirk.

I tried to say something witty, but my mouth wouldn't work, so I grinned and waved like a dork. He winked, and I watched him drive away until his car vanished beyond the building.

16

———————

AFTERGLOW

When I got home, I tried to be productive, making it as far as wiping down the kitchen counters. An hour later, dishes were still stacked in the sink, and dirty laundry was still piled in the corner of my bedroom.

My cheeks were getting sore from the unbearable grin that had only grown throughout the evening. I could barely contain myself. The poor den carpet, desperate to avoid my frantic pacing, lay flatter than a dog's ears. All I could see when I closed my eyes were Ryan's lips, his perfect teeth, his nipple teasing me as it snuck out of his tank top. That made more than my heart stir.

Completely distracted and unable to focus on even the simplest task, I tossed the rag on the counter and bounded across the room. Dwayne answered my call after one ring. I told him to hang on a second and, without waiting for his response, pressed the button to add a third person. I'd never done a three-way call and I hoped I hadn't just lost him. It took Connie three rings to answer. Then I held my breath and clicked the button again to unite all of us in telephonic bliss.

I sat on the couch and took a long breath. "Dwayne, you there?"

"I'm here."

"Connie?"

"Hi, barrier," her perky voice sang through the receiver.

"Very funny. Connie, meet Dwayne. Dwayne, Connie."

"Hi, Connie," Dwayne said. "This is either really good or really bad for him to need us both."

Connie giggled. "He's way too bubbly for it to be bad—which means this should be juicy."

Dwayne snorted.

"Are you two done?"

"Sorry, forgot this was all about you," Dwayne chided playfully.

"Go on, little one. Out with it. What have you done?" Connie took on a slightly sarcastic, motherly tone.

"I'm very much *in like*. This one's special. I mean—"

"Hang on. Back up. Who are we talking about here?" Dwayne asked.

"Did you go on your golf date with Ryan?" Connie's voice was all bubbles and excitement, pretty much her norm.

"Ryan is his name, and yes, I just got home from our date."

"Just got home? Weren't you meeting him around eleven this morning?" I could *hear* Connie grinning.

"Who's Ryan?" Dwayne asked.

"I feel like a ping-pong ball," I said.

"Wait, I thought you said you played golf with him." Dwayne now sounded baffled.

Connie giggled.

"Alright, you two. Let me tell you my story and then you can pummel me with questions. I knew getting you both on the phone was a bad idea."

Connie laughed again. "I think it's the best thing you've done all day—unless you got laid. That would definitely be the best thing, especially considering how big you thought Ryan's—"

"There was no getting laid!" Connie let out a mocking whimper at that declaration. I felt out of breath, and I'd hardly spoken.

"But he has a big cock?" Dwayne chimed in, no doubt realizing how flustered I was and loving every moment.

I let out a huff. "I have no idea how big his cock is. I've never seen it, except through his exceptionally tight jeans."

"Told you!" Connie perked back up.

"Yes, you did." I couldn't repress the smile she ignited. "Here's the short version. We met to play putt-putt. That was fun, even if he won on the last shot. Then he suggested we get lunch at the complex's café. After an hour or so, he challenged me to pool, which we played for a couple hours. He realized we'd been there all day and had to leave. We said goodbye in the parking lot, and I watched him drive off. That's it."

"Didn't you start this whole conversation with 'I'm going to marry him?' or some other nonsense?" Dwayne asked.

"Yeah, did he propose in the parking lot? When's the wedding? And when do we get to see

his—"

"Connie!"

"Wait. Did he get you a ring? I can't wait to see it! Is it huge? Or do you get a diamond-studded cock ring instead? I'm unclear on gay protocol for a proposal. I might enjoy seeing you try that on too."

"CONNIE!"

Dwayne was giggling uncontrollably now. This was hopeless.

I stood and began pacing, testing the limits of the phone's scrunchy cord.

"I don't know how I know. I just do. Ryan's amazing. We talked and laughed for hours without there ever being an awkward pause or anything. It felt like we'd known each other for years, like we were *supposed* to be together. I know that sounds nuts, but I can't remember ever feeling this before."

"Even with Carter?" Dwayne ventured.

A week ago, that name would've doused any possible exuberance. Following our breakup, it had taken weeks for me to talk about Carter and the boys without breaking down. He'd been special in a way only a first love could be; and those boys, they were *everything*.

But today, in the afterglow of the most magical, dreamy date ever, there was no blanket wet enough to douse my excitement.

"Carter was different. He was my first, and I didn't know what I was doing."

"And you do now?" Dwayne prodded.

"No, not really," I admitted. "But I *know* this is different. Everything about it *feels* different. I just left Ryan, and all I can think about is talking to him again."

"Huh," Dwayne grunted.

"Huh, what? That's never good."

"Talk? That's what you want to do with him again?"

"Yeah, I feel like I know so much about him from all our online chats, but every time we talk, I still learn so many new things. It's like unwrapping the sexiest, funniest, snarkiest present again and again—and each time it's a little different, and better."

"Dwayne?" Connie finally spoke again.

"Yeah?"

"This is bad. You know that, right? We might need an intervention," she said.

"Intervention? What are you talking about?" I asked.

Without missing a beat, Connie said, "He wants to *talk* with another gay man, and he hasn't even seen how big his—"

"Connie!"

"—cock is." She would *not* be deterred. "This coming from the guy who needs to oil the bearings in his neck from all the swiveling. Have you ever driven anywhere with him?"

Dwayne laughed.

I couldn't find words.

"I mean, really—if it's male and showing even a hint of skin, Periscope Michael is on it, locked and loaded. We can barely go fifty yards without him yelling, 'Ooh, look at that one,' or 'Did you see him?'"

"I can't help—"

"Zttt." She silenced me. "Let the grown-ups speak."

Dwayne fell into a fit of laughter, snorting through the phone.

"Something suspicious is going on with this Ryan guy." Connie went on. "Not once in this conversation have you talked about his arms or chest or butt—or anything physical. That's *very* unlike you, Michael Reed. In fact, I didn't think it was even possible. If I didn't know better, I'd suggest we drive to the emergency room right this minute to have your head examined. I'm afraid you may be *smitten*, and that's a very serious condition."

I let out an exasperated, slightly amused sigh. "That's what I've been *trying* to tell you."

17

———

LET THE GAMES BEGIN

I hung up the phone, torn between the giddy feeling that lingered from my date and the perpetual chuckle from the conversation with Connie and Dwayne. Either of them could plant a smile on my face. Together, they were a force of nature. But they both loved me and only wanted me to be happy. In Dwayne's case, paternalism might take that a step farther into 'what's best for me' territory, but the principle was the same. They were the best friends—no, the best *family*—I could ever imagine. I was lucky to have them in my life.

My stomach rumbled, and I realized it was well past dinner time. After a depressing search of my sparsely stocked kitchen, I drove to pick up some well-earned Chinese takeout. Nothing said "amazing date" like crab Rangoon.

Thirty minutes later, I was sitting in my den, oblivious to whatever show was on TV, lost in the bliss of cashew chicken and daydreams of Ryan bending over to putt. I closed my eyes, savoring a bite, and the curve of his taut lats peeking out the side of his tank top gave me a shiver. My mental eye roamed up to his exposed chest and the glistening sweat my conscious mind hadn't registered earlier. Apparently, my unconscious mind had a better eye for detail. I wanted to lick that sweat so badly. I could taste the salt.

Wait, that was a cashew.

I threw myself back on the couch and realized I'd become hard just visualizing Ryan. That *never* happened. My motor needed to be primed—and touched—before it roared to life. The idea of an image, mental or otherwise, bringing Little Michael to full attention was unheard of. Out of stupid lizard-brain curiosity, I unbuttoned my jeans and pulled the zipper down. Lo and behold, Little Michael popped up faster than a Jack-in-the-Box. I chuckled at that thought, then realized the double entendre of *Jack*.

That made me harder.

Getting harder made me think about Ryan.

My hand, still greasy from the Rangoon, grazed the tip of my penis. It quivered. I closed my eyes and replayed every hole, imagining Ryan walking, bending, stretching, and flexing. His tank top blew in the breeze. A gust came along and somehow—in the way unexplained things happen in dreams—it vanished, leaving him standing bare chested, putter in hand.

I had my putter in hand too. Stroke after stroke.

I watched him squeeze the shaft of his club, gripping and releasing, sliding his hands up and down. He knelt to line up his shot and his jeans cupped his perfectly round ass. Blond hair blew in the breeze, and I could smell his musk, a delicious mixture of sweat, heat, and Irish Spring. Damn, those leprechauns knew how to make soap.

Satisfied, he stood, fiddling the club with his fingers, rubbing it, making it his. He *owned* that club. I felt him own it. I felt him own me, want me, love me. He needed me. I knew it. He had to have me, to stroke me, to stroke—

Then, without warning, he putted, and the ball shot through the clown's mouth—I mean, face—I mean, into the hole.

Dammit.

I had shot all over my cashew chicken.

If I hadn't been so turned on by the scene in my mind, I would've been horrified by the desecration of my favorite meal, but it was worth it. Ryan might not have realized it, but we'd just come together for the first time.

Alright, it was in my head, but in my own weird way, I was admitting to myself just how bad I had it for this guy.

Connie was right. I was *smitten.*

Spent, mentally and physically, my mind returned to the present. I stared up at the ceiling, grinning like an idiot, wishing Ryan had been there to take his shot for real.

Pick your entendre. I wanted them all, as long as they were his.

***

SATURDAY 9:51 P.M.

HEY YOU. I REALLY HAD A GREAT TIME TODAY. THAT WAS SUPPOSED TO BE A QUICK ROUND OF PUTT-PUTT, BUT I COULDN'T STAND THE IDEA OF GOING OUR SEPARATE WAYS SO QUICKLY. THANKS FOR GIVING ME A WHOLE DAY. YOU LOOKED SUPER SEXY, BY THE WAY.

I HAVE TO GO OUT OF TOWN TOMORROW FOR WORK AND WILL BE GONE ALL WEEK. CAN I SEE YOU NEXT WEEKEND? DINNER, MAYBE? POOL REMATCH, SINCE YOU CRUSHED MY HOPES AND DREAMS?

. . .

LET'S TALK ONLINE THIS WEEK WHILE I'M GONE.

THINKING OF YOU (AND SMILING).

RYAN

I REALLY DON'T KNOW HOW LONG I STARED AT THE monitor, drinking in every word of that email. The goofy grin never left my face. Ryan was thinking about me—and wanted to see me again. That made my heart go into hyper-drive. This was real. I wasn't imagining things. This amazing, funny, smart, successful, insanely hot guy—with poochy lips —liked *me*.

I grinned wider, thinking about his lower lip protruding before him. It had seemed like such an annoying flaw when we'd first met, something that distracted from his other, more delicious qualities. Now, as I saw that lip in my mind's eye, my chest warmed. It was cute. It was part of him, something no one else had. I wanted to kiss that lip.

"Shit, you're sappy," I said to myself, chuckling at my own schmaltziness. "But you can't leave him hanging on such a great email. How does a smitten puppy respond without sounding so…smitten?"

SATURDAY 10:02 P.M.

HEY YOU BACK.

TODAY WAS ONE OF THE BEST DATES I'VE EVER HAD. REALLY. PUTT-PUTT WAS A BLAST (EVEN IF YOU CHEATED ON THAT LAST SHOT *CHUCKLE*), AND ALL THE OTHER STUFF WAS FUN TOO. I STILL CAN'T BELIEVE WE NEVER RUN OUT OF THINGS TO TALK ABOUT. IS THAT NORMAL?

WHAT KIND OF BUSINESS TRIP ARE YOU GOING ON? WHERE WILL YOU BE? INQUIRING MINDS…

YES, LET'S DO DINNER NEXT WEEKEND. AND YES, LET'S IM AND EMAIL. YOU MAKE ME SMILE.

OH, DID I MENTION THAT TANK TOP WAS INDUCTED INTO THE DATING HALL OF FAME? I WAS HAVING NAUGHTY THOUGHTS ALL NIGHT THANKS TO YOU.

REALLY NAUGHTY THOUGHTS. WAY TO RUIN THIS RIGHTEOUS PK, MISTER *GRIN*.

ENOUGH OF THAT. HAVE A GREAT TRIP. CAN'T WAIT TO SEE YOU NEXT WEEK.

M

AS I WAS REREADING MY EMAIL FOR THE THIRD TIME after sending it, giggling at my own cleverness, Mr. AOL announced, "You've Got Mail."

Ryan had replied.

I turned into a thirteen-year-old girl with her first school crush, hopping out of my chair and wiggling in a weird white-man happy dance before plopping back into the chair. I sat with my feet tucked under my butt and leaned toward the screen—as if his message would hop out and kiss me or something.

SATURDAY 10:03 P.M.

. . .

You had naughty thoughts about me? I love that. Why don't you do something about it? Unzip and take care of yourself thinking about me. That would be so hot.

I'm a Scorpio. I like it hot and hard. What can I say?

Enjoy yourself.

Ryan

I laughed as I read his message. If he only knew what I'd already done to my poor Chinese takeout in his name…

18

STOP THINK!ING

As the leaves of Atlanta began to turn, days at Think! started feeling like one long battle. Ted was an irritable boss, and his cadre of yes-men rarely challenged his holy word. Connie and I had been hired to change the culture within the sales and recruiting teams, but Ted undermined our progress by issuing ridiculous edicts born out of bad information or knee-jerk reactions.

"You're not going to believe what His Majesty did today."

Connie covered her mouth with a finger. "Shh. Not so loud."

"Sorry," I whispered. We were sitting in my office, but she had a point. The walls were thin.

"He made my entire team stand."

She quirked a brow. "Stand? You mean stand up?"

"Yeah, and *keep* standing. He said he'd been looking over the outbound call numbers and wasn't happy. He thinks the team's been lazy about making their dials."

"So he made them stand up? That doesn't make any sense."

"He didn't just make them stand up. He took away their chairs for the entire morning—from eight o'clock until lunch. They had to dial and talk while standing at their desks."

Her jaw dropped. "You're kidding."

"Nope. You want to know when I learned about this little exercise in idiocy?"

"Uh-oh."

"Traffic was a mess this morning, and I was a few minutes late. When I walked in, everyone was already on their feet. You should've seen the looks I got when I walked onto the sales floor."

"They're blaming *you*? You weren't even here when he did that."

I shrugged. "I don't know if they're really blaming me, but they look to me to shield them from him, to talk sense into him before he pulls shit like this. Before you and I came along, he'd do things like this almost daily."

She put her head in her hands. "He can't do this. It undermines everything we've been working for."

"Yeah, I know."

"Have you talked to him about it?"

"I tried. He blew me off, said he had appointments this morning. He suggested I join him and the boys for lunch."

She snorted. "You mean the daily lunch where they make all the decisions? The one I'm never invited to?"

"You and me both. And yes, *that* lunch." I blew out a breath. "I've been here, what, five months? Six? We haven't had a single management team meeting. Everything gets decided at lunch where neither of our teams are represented. We find out our marching orders later and have to clean up their mess."

We sat in silence staring at the surface of my dusty desk.

"I don't know how long I can keep doing this," I whispered, more to myself than to her.

She stood slowly. "Go to lunch. See if they'll listen. You've got to at least try."

I nodded. She was right, but I failed to see what difference it would make. Ted didn't listen to anyone other than Mark and Dennis. As Connie left my office, I realized how awkward that conversation must've been for her. She'd only been with the company for a couple months, and I was the person who brought her into the fold. We were equals, partners in leading the bulk of the company's employees, and she'd never seen me show anything other than an upbeat and positive attitude. What would she think now? The idea of my team suffering under Ted's stupidity drove me crazy, but the thought of letting Connie down stung deeper.

Mark's giant form darkened my door and snapped me out of my thoughts. "Hey, you look too serious. Come to lunch. I think the boss is buying barbecue."

Mark was a good guy. He rarely said a negative word, and was an incredible salesman. I had thought he'd take a back seat when he stepped out of management to focus on his own sales efforts, but Ted insisted he continue going to lunch every day. Not only was Ted making critical decisions at those lunches, but he also sought the input of his *former* sales manager rather than his current sales manager.

The last thing I wanted to do was to stink like barbecue, but I smiled and stood. "Sounds great, especially if it's on Ted."

Mark chuckled. "Absolutely. Come on. You can ride with me."

A LITTLE AFTER FOUR O'CLOCK, CONNIE STRODE INTO my office and plopped into a chair.

"So, how was lunch? Love that new cologne you're wearing. What is it? Aux de Piggy?"

"Ha ha. Very funny." I sniffed my shirt and wrinkled my nose. "Argh. That's terrible."

She snorted.

"Lunch was about what you'd expect. The guys talked about nothing until the food came, then Ted launched into the numbers. He was *pissed* about the call stats. I tried to point out that our sales and net revenue numbers were breaking all-time records, but he wouldn't hear it. All he cared about was how many dials per day each salesperson made. At one point, Mark tried to back me up, but Ted blew him off. He threatened to make the entire team stand until every salesperson hits a hundred dials in the same day."

"What?" She sat back. "He can't do that. If we had an HR person, they'd go nuts. Besides, is that even possible, every person hitting a hundred?"

"Of course it's not. If they get a hot lead on the phone, that one call could take thirty minutes. The better salespeople spend most of their time on the phone, but only talk to a dozen or so people per day. If someone makes a hundred dials, they're either not reaching anyone, or they suck at closing. More dials won't fix either of those problems."

"What are you going to do?" she asked.

"I don't know." Without thinking, I started

fiddling with a pen, clicking it over and over. "You've been here long enough to see how things are. Do you think he'll ever change?"

She thought a moment. "I don't know. Probably not. He built this place from scratch. He's proud of it —hell, he's just proud."

"That's an understatement." I rolled my eyes. "He deserves credit for getting this place to twenty million, but he'll never take it to the next level pulling crap like this. I had three of my team threaten to quit today if he made them stand again."

"Really?"

I nodded.

We both jumped at a knock on my door. It was Evan, one of my sales guys.

Connie craned her neck, then stood. "I'll let you deal with Skippy." That was her nickname for Evan. He was a strong closer, but had a quirky personality that always left me wondering if he'd stood a little too close to the microwave as a kid.

I chuckled. "Okay. Thanks for listening. Sorry to dump on you like this."

She waved me off and opened the door. "He's all yours," she said to Evan.

When Connie vanished down the hallway, Evan closed the door, sat on the edge of the chair, and leaned forward.

"I'm giving you my notice."

Shit. "Evan, you're one of my best guys, and you've only been here a few months. Why would you want to leave?"

He sat back and crossed his arms. "I won't stand and dial, or whatever lunacy Lord Think! comes up with next."

I raised my palms in surrender. "I know—"

"Everybody out there knows *you* didn't do this, that you would never do this, but we also know you can only talk so much sense into Ted. Those who've been around a lot longer than me say this is how he's always been. They don't think he'll ever change. I wouldn't be surprised if half the sales team left over the next few months." He sucked in a deep breath, then lowered his voice to a whisper. "Look, I didn't come in here to discuss this. My mind's made up. I'm leaving. The only question is whether you're coming with me or not."

I might've been raised by wolves, but I wasn't easily shocked—well, unless you counted the acrobatic positions and fetishes I was learning about on Manhunt or AOL—but those weren't on the agenda for this meeting. My jaw must've dropped to my desk because Evan was grinning from ear to ear.

"What, uh, you want me to—what?"

"I want you to come with me. Get out of this

place. The old crowd is right. Ted's never going to change, and we can do better without him."

I barely knew what to think, much less say. "What are you talking about?"

"I found this company out west. They teach people how to be computer engineers, help them get their Microsoft certification. They're willing to give me the rights to sell in the eastern US. I'm a decent sales guy, but I don't know how to run a business. I need someone like you to make this work. I want you to be my business partner."

I stared at him, trying to see if he was pulling my leg—or setting me up. Ted had been known to test people like this. He called it "checking their loyalty."

Ted was such an asshole.

"Evan, I don't know what to say. I mean, I'm flattered you'd think of me, but—"

He threw up a hand, staving off my objections. "I get it. It's a lot to take in, and I caught you off guard. You don't need to make a decision right now. Let me get you the information on the company and the business plan I came up with. If you like what you see, we can talk more. We're not doing anything but talking about a hypothetical business transaction. Are you okay with that?"

I hesitated. What was I doing? This was nuts. Ted might be an ass, but he ran a successful, stable company. He'd given me a job the same week I'd moved to Atlanta. Hell, Think! was the reason I had a comfortable life in a new town I absolutely loved. And Evan was asking me to throw all that away, for what—a startup?

Then again, my time working with my dad taught me how much I enjoyed the independence of working for myself. Maybe owning a company with a partner would be a good thing.

Despite the churning in my gut, I looked up at him and nodded once. "Alright, but you can't give me your notice today. Don't do that until you're ready to leave and start this new thing. If I decide to join you, we'll have to figure out how to time things."

He smiled. "I'm good with that. Consider my resignation rescinded." He stood. "This is gonna be awesome. You'll see."

As soon as he vanished from my doorway, I grabbed the phone and dialed Connie's extension. "Emergency dinner. Now."

She laughed. "Did you see another barrier? Are we going to say hi to it?"

I couldn't hold back my own laugh. "Yeah, a big one—just not the kind you're thinking."

"ARE YOU REALLY CONSIDERING THIS?" CONNIE asked between sips of pinot grigio. Why she put ice cubes in wine baffled me. I wasn't an expert on alcohol consumption, but that offended even my rookie sense of liquor honor.

"I don't know." I set my fork down and leaned back, staring at the ceiling fan as it spun lazily above. "I love working with you, and I really like our teams. We've done some great work."

"Chez Paris!" she said with a terrible French accent and a wave of her hand.

"Oui, Paris." I said in my best Tennessee-drawl-infected French accent. "The idea of leaving you makes me sick, but Evan's right. Ted's a raging prick, and that's never going to change. They do their lunch every day and make decisions for our teams without including us, then he pulls crap like the standing calls. I can't blame the troops for looking at the door with that shit going on."

"Yeah, the recruiters were talking, wondering when he'd do it to them."

"If we start losing people, you know who Ted will blame, don't you? Mr. High Holy created this company and shits gold. He'll pin it all on you and me. Then where will we be?"

She eyed me over her glass, one brow raised. "Are

you venting or trying to convince yourself of something?"

I sighed. "I don't know. Connie, he's *terrible*. I can't see myself at Think! in three years. If I'm honest, I couldn't see myself there in a year, with or without Evan's deal. I haven't seriously looked for something else, but when sales manager jobs have posted for clients, I've caught myself wondering if I might be a good fit for them."

"Well, it sounds like you've decided, at least about leaving. The only question is where you'll go."

This was usually the time Connie made a joke or used a silly voice to lighten the mood. She did neither. She just sat across the table waiting for the lightbulb to go off in my stubborn, thick skull.

I lowered my head. "I guess. This really sucks. I was looking forward to doing more things like Paris with you. We're a great team."

She beamed. "No, we're the best. Ted's lucky to have us, even if his head's too far up his ass to see it."

"Ms. Black. Language, please," I mocked.

"Oh, forgive me, kind sir. I will watch my fucking language for you in the future."

Just like that, the tension broke and we were giggling like children again.

A FEW DAYS LATER, EVAN RECEIVED A PACKET OF information from the owners of the training company in Utah, two guys who started the business out of one of their garages and now boasted several million dollars in annual sales. The only small business I knew by comparison was my dad's wholesale drug distributor, which barely sold half a million dollars of product each year. Ted claimed Think! brought in roughly twenty million each year. If Evan and I could get this thing off the ground and generate revenues somewhere in the middle of those two extremes, I'd be thrilled.

Over the weeks that followed, Evan and I held dozens of clandestine meetings, usually over lunch so we wouldn't raise suspicion among the Think! crowd. I told Connie what was going on, but no one else knew anything was amiss. Part of me hoped Ted would take the advice of everyone and stop the tyrannical shenanigans, but he never did. Chairs went missing on occasion, and call stats were posted several times each day to humiliate those with lower numbers. Morale among the troops, which I had doubted could get any lower, found a way to limbo under even those minimal expectations.

People were miserable.

Four weeks following the Great Chair Removal,

the first salesperson resigned. Two more left the following week.

Ted was incensed. He couldn't wrap his head around why people would leave his blessed company. Behind closed doors, he ranted to his inner circle about how those leaving were betraying him, after everything he'd done for them. Never once did he look in the mirror and ask, "What is really causing people to leave?"

He took his anger out on anyone nearby, either with snide remarks or outright attacks on their performance or professionalism. Even Mark, Ted's most loyal and long-standing employee, fell prey to his biting barbs.

Morale went from poor to pathetic. The rumor mill predicted a wave of resignations in the coming weeks. Connie and I did all we could to encourage people, but we could no longer buffer the troops from Ted's tantrums.

Late one Thursday afternoon, Evan walked into my office and closed the door behind him.

"I can't do this anymore. Ted's an ass, and we have all we need to start the new company."

"We need capital. We can't start a company without cash. I can't afford to go without a paycheck right now." I had less than a thousand dollars in my bank account. I might've been a good sales manager, but I was a terrible saver.

"I have some money saved up. I'll invest twenty thousand to get us started. The company can pay me back when we turn a profit."

I gaped at him. He was offering to fund our startup out of his own pocket. I knew Evan's family had money, but I didn't think he enjoyed any of it yet. Then again, I wasn't exactly an expert on trust funds. All I'd likely inherit from my family was debt.

"Evan, I can't—"

"Yes, you can. Please. I can't do this without you. Cash or no cash, without someone to run the business, to connect us to lenders and handle the day-to-day, I'll be lost. I need you."

I stared down at my hands for a long moment, barely breathing. It felt like one of those life moments where I could see the fork in the road stretching for miles before me. Neither path showed any hint of the destination or ease of travel. I begged that vision to offer some message, some hint, but nothing came.

"Can I sleep on it and give you an answer tomorrow?" I finally asked.

He grinned and bounced toward the door. "Sure. Bring your resignation letter."

I sat at my desk for another hour, staring but not seeing. One coworker after another trailed past, waving goodnight but not waiting for the reply that wouldn't come. My stomach clenched as I thought through my options for the thousandth time.

One: I stay the course with Think! and try to make things better with Ted. That wouldn't be an easy road, but it offered stability and a paycheck. More than that, Connie was there, and I loved working with her. We'd be friends no matter where I worked, but I'd miss seeing her every day and collaborating on crazy contests and whatnot.

Two: I leave and find a new job. I hadn't even looked at the job market, and the thought of starting over scared me. Plus, in the time I'd been at Think!, I'd learned a lot about résumés and the impact that single sheet of paper had on an employer's decision. I might be able to explain having a rough start in Atlanta with my first job, but I'd still have to explain it in *every* interview. That sounded terrible.

The third option was to take Evan up on his offer and start a new company. That was the scariest of all, but also the most exciting. It got me away from Ted and made me my own boss. I liked Evan well enough, and the Utah company had checked out. They even offered to help support us in the startup phase. All the proverbial ducks were lined up and waiting for me to have the balls to lead them.

THE NEXT MORNING, I WALKED INTO THINK! FOR THE last time, gave Evan a nod, and took my resignation letter down to Ted's office. He blew a total gasket and refused my offer for a transition period. He even forced Mark and Dennis to escort me out the door, like one of those perp walks you might see on TV murder shows. I held my head high as the troops gathered and applauded my exit. Evan had told them what I was doing in Ted's office.

I hated thinking about what spite-filled punishment Ted would hand out for that little display of disloyalty.

But I was free.

19

SLUTISHA, PARTY OF ONE

With one job over and the other yet to begin, I found myself with a little time on my hands.

While I kept my daily evening ritual of purchasing a singular apple, working out, eating Chinese or grilled chicken at Cowtippers, then heading home, my days were free for other important pursuits: the men of Atlanta.

I checked my email each night and was disappointed there was nothing from Ryan. He hadn't called, but that wasn't unusual. He was an emailer. It was strange he'd just vanished without even a quick note after the fantastic day we'd had, but I shrugged it off as a busy man on a work trip.

At least, that's what I hoped it was.

Could he not have had the same post-date

euphoria I'd had? It wouldn't have been the first time I'd misjudged a guy's reaction. Hell, I was usually so optimistic after a date, I assumed the dude was picking out rings or picket fences. Wait, that's lesbians. Maybe he'd just be thinking about me and our next date. Yeah, that's more like it.

Despite my newfound hope for something more with Ryan, experience had taught me to hedge my bets. The odds of any one date turning into a long-lasting love affair were slim, especially when you slammed the egos, stunted emotions, and general horniness of two men together.

Given that world-class rationalization, I turned my free time toward mastering Manhunt and Adam4Adam, while not shirking my fans on AOL. One must care for one's followers, after all.

Yes, I was a bit of a slut.

And I loved Atlanta.

With a few clicks of my mouse, a horny, half-dressed man would show up at my door faster than a pizza from Domino's. Over the past few months, I'd learned to weed out those who lived in Monroe Place, my home. I'd made the mistake of hooking up with a *homer*, and was thoroughly embarrassed when we ran into each other at the pool or laundry room. That was a shame, really. The convenience of having so many men within walking distance was appealing.

As you might imagine, the little angel and devil appeared each time I "ordered in." They fought like an old married couple, or like the two old guys on the balcony from *The Muppet Show*—yeah, that's more like it. The angel played the Ryan card, begging me to be good and have faith that he'd show up and sweep me off my feet, but the devil made a more compelling, immediate argument. Little Michael had an itch and might fall off if I didn't scratch it.

That was probably not medically possible, but it worked in the moment. My entry into slutdom was pure self-preservation. I couldn't exactly let Little Michael wither and drop, could I?

On Thursday night, as I scrolled through the menu—er, I mean, the men online—my PC let out a familiar ding. I closed the Manhunt browser, then minimized A4A, revealing a lonely, untended AOL screen beneath. I'd pretty much abandoned the chat rooms for the pictures and profiles of the dating sites. They contained the same guys, just with different goals and timetables. How's that for rationalization?

RAL2027: HEY YOU! HOW'S YOUR WEEK BEEN?

Wow, that was fast. He'd logged on and messaged me right away. I felt a little flutter.

IT'S BEEN OKAY. HOW'S THE TRIP? YOU'RE IN LA?

SAN FRAN. IT'S OKAY. SAME OLE.

San Francisco? The gay Mecca? I'd never been there, but every movie I'd ever seen depicted the city as one massive orgy, with hairy, muscular men pounding each other in rapid succession. While the mental imagery might've thrilled me a moment ago, my heart sank at the thought of Ryan being there all week.

Oh, never been there, I replied, unable to leave it alone.

It's okay. Our office is downtown, and my hotel is right across the street. It's convenient, but I don't do much more than work, eat, and sleep.

That was a little reassuring. Ryan being bored and a workaholic was good, right?

Oh, cool, I guess.

You alright? You seem a little…I don't know…*off*.

Yeah, I'm good. Just been a long week. Lots going on at work.

Why was I *off*, as he put it? I felt it too. Talking with Ryan had never been uncomfortable or awkward. In fact, he might've been the easiest person I'd ever talked with. Tonight, I felt like a sputtering idiot.

Poof. "It's because you've been hooking up with other guys while he's away on a work trip. You're a trollop, Michael. Face it." The little angel wore a black pilgrim outfit with white lace crawling up his neck. Since when did male pilgrims wear lace?

"Don't listen to that prude. You and Ryan have been on exactly *two* dates. You don't owe him anything. Have your fun." The little devil, wearing brown chaps without underwear, wagged a finger at me. "You don't want Little Michael falling off, remember?"

The angel sighed.

Was I feeling guilty? That was a stupid question. PKs were always feeling guilty about *something*.

The angel was right, I had been slutting my way around Atlanta while poor Ryan was working.

Shit. Now I *knew* I felt guilty.

STILL THERE?

The cursor blinked impatiently.

OH, SORRY. RAN TO THE KITCHEN. SO, WHEN ARE YOU HOME?

FRIDAY. I WANTED TO SEE IF YOU'D HAVE LUNCH WITH ME SATURDAY. I CAN'T MAKE IT A DAY LIKE LAST TIME, BUT I CAN DEFINITELY SQUEEZE IN A LUNCH.

Squeeze in a lunch? Was his social secretary keeping him that busy? Sheesh.

SURE. I'D LOVE TO. NAME THE TIME AND PLACE.

He suggested a Thai place I hadn't heard of. I

looked up the address and agreed on noon, then he said he had to take a phone call and logged off.

It was 10:15 p.m. Who was calling him at ten fifteen on a Thursday night while he was on a work trip? I wasn't exactly hearing an alarm bell, but there was an uncomfortable feeling creeping up my spine. Then I chided myself for being jealous of a man I had no claim over—as if anyone ever has a claim on anyone else. Then I scolded myself for that notion.

Wow. I'd just completed a guilt hat trick.

I was a damn good PK. My father would be proud.

THAI FOOD HAS ALWAYS BEEN ONE OF MY FAVORITES. There's something comforting and rich in the flavors and aromas that makes me happy.

As I sat across from Ryan, my stomach rumbled at the thought of pad Thai. Nothing said love like peanuty goodness.

"How was San Fran?" I asked between chews of veggie spring roll.

"Fine," he said, brushing the crumbs from his fingers. "It's always the same: corporate bosses asking questions about reports, a steady stream of issues with our travel vendors, and some new vendor banging on the door wanting our business. That pretty much sums up every day, now that I think about it. Oh, I can't forget dealing with employees. It's a rare day that I don't have at least one employee calling to complain about Delta or American—or Amtrak. I catch more flack about them than all the others combined."

"Amtrak? The trains?" I was travel-challenged and had never been on a train.

He nodded. "They're comfortable if you're in a room with a bed, but for the average traveler stuck in the front, it can make for a really long ride—and anyone who tells you those trips are smooth is lying. Trains rattle and sway, especially if you're on the top car."

"Huh. People complain to you about that? What do they want you to do?"

He chuckled. "No clue. Mostly, they want to vent, for someone to listen. I do that, then tell them I'll talk to our corporate rep about their concerns. That calms most down. They don't really expect me to work miracles."

Corporate America. I envied the stability and fat paycheck that came with Ryan's high-end white-collar gig, but parts of it sounded like a real pain. I thought about all the issues I'd been dealing with at Think!, a small company basically run by one man, then I tried to imagine answering to thousands of bosses and coworkers, a board of directors and investors, and I realized his fat paycheck came with some sharply barbed strings.

"How was your week?" he asked.

"Ehh. It was okay."

He cocked his head. "Just okay? You're usually more upbeat than that. Did something happen? What did Ted do now?"

I nearly spit the hot tea I'd started to sip. How had he known Ted was at it again? Then I remembered all our online chats and realized he knew more about me than most third dates. Hell, he knew more about me that anyone I'd ever dated. That realization slapped me in the face. I thought it was a good slap, the kind you get on your butt right before—

"How did you know?" I gave him a wan smile. "I don't know how much more of his nonsense I can take. He made my whole team stand while they did calls. He actually took their chairs, moved them into the conference room until his little object lesson was complete."

"You're kidding?"

"Nope. Sad but true."

"Wow. He's a real ass."

I nodded. "My exact words to Connie."

His face lightened at the mention of my new bestie's name. "How is dear Connie? Any more French flags flying about?"

Damn, he didn't miss anything, did he?

"No more flags. She's good. Chipper as ever, though Ted's stunt burst her usual bubbliness for a hot minute."

He sobered again. "If Ted's so bad, why stay? You're a bright guy. You could find something else."

He thought I was bright. My cheeks colored at his flattery.

"So, it's funny you say that. One of my sales guys came to me with an opportunity." I took a sip of tea to give myself time to think. Ryan was a successful business guy. Would he think I was crazy considering a startup? Would I look unstable? The last thing I wanted was for him to think I was a flake or didn't know how to stick to things.

He raised a brow as I struggled for words.

"There's a guy at work, one of my sales guys. His name's Evan. He has a connection to this company somewhere out west that provides Microsoft certification training to engineers."

"So it's a school? Or a for-profit educational institution?"

"Right. It's definitely a company, not a school. Evan's supposed to get more details next week. All he had when he approached me was an overview and the offer to take the eastern US. They're not even asking him to buy the rights."

"Huh." Ryan leaned back and one hand drifted to his mouth.

"Okay," I said. "In sales, we call that gesture a *stop sign*, and it's usually used by prospects when they don't like something. What are you thinking?"

He grinned at my grilling. "IT is a hot field, that's for sure, but we still don't know enough to get a handle on the business. I'd be interested to hear what Evan comes up with this week. Until then, it's just an idea. We can't make a plan with just an idea."

Ryan was a good dozen years older than me. In that moment, I felt our age difference for the first time. He sounded so intelligent and experienced, so stable. I could see his mind working as his eyes drifted upward, then back to me. He was trying to puzzle out the scraps of information I'd given him, trying to find a way to make things work.

And then I realized he'd used the word *we*. Sure, he was just talking about an idea someone had presented, but he talked as though *we* were making a decision together.

That made me smile.

Ryan noticed the change. "What are you grinning at, mister?"

"Oh, nothing." I decided to play it cool. "I just appreciate you helping me think through all this. It's a big decision to leave a company and do something new."

"It is, but I admire you for considering it."

"You do?" The flutter grew stronger.

He nodded. "It takes a lot of guts to leave the safety of a company and start something. Most people fail when they start a business, but you won't be one of them."

Sweet mother of pearl. He *believed* in me. I had to fight the urge to do a happy dance. My guts were already doing one.

"Thanks," I squeaked, before taking a quick sip to wet my suddenly parched whistle.

We spent the rest of dinner talking about little things. The Atlanta fall softball season was kicking off, and I was excited to get back on the field. I'd been assigned to a team called the Slippers. Ryan teased that I'd have to play in heels. When he asked what position I played, his brows rose again.

"Pitcher, eh. I had you pegged for another position."

I chuckled. "Really now? Are we still talking softball?"

He raised his glass. "You tell me. I love a well-rounded player."

"Let's just say I'm a *team* player."

"So, you'd let me change your position, if I wanted?"

"Put me in, coach." I saluted with my own raised glass.

His eyes sparkled, and his smile broadened as he held my gaze.

20

THE CHRISTENING

The next few weeks were a flurry of activity. Evan and I scouted new office space, settling on a building owned by a bankruptcy attorney who had a few offices to rent. We took the bottom floor, which consisted of two offices, a small conference room, a storage room for files, and a restroom. The attorney was an older lady who loved gold gilding, so the place was decked out like a French palace. There wasn't much elbow room, but it was fancy. My office contained an elegant cherry-wood desk that reflected lamplight like a mirror, along with high-back armchairs with ball-and-claw feet. It made me think of an episode of *Antiques Roadshow*, in which the blond twins had shown off dining chairs with the same feet. They were really cool.

The Utah guys put us through our paces, which

included studying software loaded onto laptops and four-inch-thick binders. My head hurt after the first day. I'd never been rocket-scientist-smart, but was brighter than the average bulb. Something in the monotony of those sessions made me wonder how dim a bulb could get. Mine was flickering like it wanted to give that lasts pop and never shine again.

I was glad Evan was handling sales because I would've thrown that binder through the window before finishing it. All I needed to know was the basics and how to explain our business to banks and other businesses.

Throughout the craziness, I maintained my post-workday ritual of stopping by the grocery store for a lonely apple, then heading to the gym. Ryan and I emailed and IMed several times each day. He was all about meeting for lunch on Saturday or Sunday, but always had some reason he couldn't do dinner. It was odd, but I was too busy to give it much thought.

On the fourth Saturday following my resignation from Think!, Ryan and I met for lunch at a diner near the new office. I was proud of our little venture and wanted to show off the fancy digs to my…what was he at this point? Date? We'd been on a dozen dates, all either lunches or coffee. We'd never been physical, though he had kissed me a couple of times. Why was that?

For once, my Pisces mind let a subject rest without hammering both sides into submission. I liked Ryan, and I was pretty sure he liked me. His *eyes* said he did. We'd been dating a couple months, that's all. It wasn't more than that. I wanted it to be, but wouldn't let myself think of it as more until it happened.

Calm down, Michael. Breathe. It's just a date.

"I can't wait to see your new place. It sounds swanky," Ryan said between bites of eggs Benedict. The diner was new to both of us, a little breakfast place called Le Peep. The sign out front pictured a fuzzy yellow chick just peeking out of a newly cracked egg. That's what drew us in. It was cute. As it turned out, the food was fantastic, and the servers were a hoot. Our server, Betty (yes, also the name of my all-time favorite Saturn), literally threw packets of sweetener at Ryan when he asked for more, then stormed off like she was mad at his insufferable request. It was all an act, part of the charm of the place, and we loved every minute.

"It really is. There's not much room, but it's enough for the two of us."

We talked about the first few weeks of training, the Utah guys and their outlook on the business, and how Evan and I planned to kick things off. Ryan listened attentively, asking questions and making suggestions throughout. It was like having my own personal business coach—a really hot coach with a tight powder-blue T-shirt that nuzzled his biceps just right.

I took a sip of iced water to cool down.

Betty eventually strode by, scolded us for not cleaning our plates more effectively, then threw the bill at Ryan. We laughed all the way out the door. Betty flicked us the bird and a broad smile.

Le Peep just became our new favorite breakfast joint.

The office was a quick five-minute drive from the restaurant, and the attorneys rarely worked weekends, so we found the place dark and locked up tight.

"Holy shit. You weren't kidding when you said the boss likes fancy gold." Ryan's head rotated, taking in the high ceilings and gilded trim. He walked across the entrance toward a graceful painting that consumed the entire far wall, then whistled. "This is an *original*. I bet she paid at least twenty thousand for it."

"Dollars?" I almost stumbled.

He turned back and nodded. "Yeah. This thing's stunning."

I showed him the conference room, then Evan's office, then took him upstairs to see the fanciest room in the building, the old attorney's private conference room. Cherry wood and polished silver gleamed throughout. A buffet held court on the far wall, donned with several massive candelabras holding tall, white, never-been-lit candles. Twenty elegant chairs lined the table at the center. Before each high-back chair sat a crystal water glass, writing pad, and pen. A faint leathery smell drifted throughout the room from the rich mats on which those items rested.

Ryan whistled again, walking to the far side to examine a vase. "Is this thing real?" he asked, kneeling down to look under it.

"No idea. Knowing the owner, probably."

He glanced around the room one last time, then we went back downstairs to my office.

"This is my little corner." I waved my hand in a flourish.

"Very nice." He skimmed the bookcase, then walked around my desk and dropped into my leather office chair. "This is comfy. Kinda bouncy."

I chuckled. "That it is."

"Does your door lock?"

"Uh, sure."

I didn't know why, but my heart started racing.

"Lock it and come over here. I want to kiss you, and I'd rather not be disturbed."

I grinned. "Yes, sir. Though I doubt anyone will come in today."

"Just do as you're told, young man." He motioned to the lock.

My grin widened.

He grabbed me around the waist when I got within arm's reach and pulled me onto his lap. It took an awkward moment of flailing legs to get me fully situated. I'm not sure how we did it, but my legs flowed over the top of the chair's arms as my butt ground into his lap. It wasn't comfortable, but I didn't dare move.

He reached up with both hands and pulled my face toward him, pressing his lips against mine in our most passionate kiss to date. His poochy lower lip devoured mine as he went from zero to sixty in two-point-three seconds.

His embrace was aggressive, but the first tickle of his tongue was tentative, questioning. It sent a shiver of warmth through my chest, and I answered with my own, exploring the underside of his.

He groaned.

All questions vanished. I'd wanted this so badly over the previous weeks that I lost myself in his embrace. My hands found their way to his chest, tracing the definition, gripping its firmness. His fingers rubbed my back, tickled my neck. The chair squeaked as he shifted, and I realized he'd hardened under the weight and grinding of my butt. I pressed myself against him, making him squirm even more.

"I want you, Michael."

"You can have whatever you want."

"I want to be inside you. Now."

I pulled my head back and quirked a brow. "Now? Here? In my office?"

He grinned and nodded. "Right here. Right now. You said it yourself—no one's coming in."

He reached down and began untying the string on my shorts.

I fumbled my way to stand before him. "You're serious?"

The only answer was the sound of my pants hitting the floor. I rarely wore underwear, so Little Michael stared up at him with curiosity in his one good eye.

Ryan gaped, then his gaze rose to meet mine. "Damn."

I helped him with his pants, amused to find he wasn't wearing undies either.

"Holy shit, that's big," I blurted out.

He chuckled. "And it's all yours. Want it?"

"Hell yeah. Although it may take me a minute."

His cock was perfect. Eight and a half inches of thick, veiny manhood, curved slightly upward and crowned with a pink, cut mushroom tip that begged to be licked.

I never got the chance.

Ryan gripped my hips with both hands and pulled me into his mouth, taking Little Michael all the way to my balls before I knew what was happening.

Damn, he didn't even gag.

My whole body convulsed.

Ever so gently, he pulled back, running his lips along my shaft and his tongue around the rim of my head. He kept the tip in his mouth and toyed with it, alternating between his teeth and his tongue. Despite his iron grip on my hips, I had to brace myself on the desk. My office was spinning.

When I stiffened to my limit, he switched to slowly swallowing my dick, tracing it gently with his teeth, taking all of me with each motion.

Then he stopped and leaned back. "Take off your shirt."

In one perfume-commercial-like movement, I gripped the bottom of my shirt, yanked it over my head, and tossed it into the corner.

Ryan's eyes widened appreciatively as he reached up to trace my still-forming abs. "So nice."

I blushed. "Thanks."

He chuckled. "I like that you get embarrassed. It makes me want you more."

The reddening deepened. "And *your* shirt?"

He leaned forward in the chair and removed his tee, revealing the most beautifully sculpted chest and shoulders I'd ever seen—and I'd seen some beauties in my short little slut-life. His pecs were full enough to actually cast a shadow. I couldn't speak. I just stared.

"You can do more than look. It's all yours."

I couldn't believe this was happening. Ryan was amazing: smart, hot, successful, and he wanted *me*—in my office. I kept waiting to wake up from the dream or for someone to knock on the door, but neither happened. Then my eyes shot toward the door and a thrill ran through me at the possibility of getting caught. What were we doing—in my office? What if one of the attorneys or their staff walked in? What if Evan showed up? *He had a key.*

Excitement at dancing with danger overrode good sense, and I turned back with hunger in my eyes.

Ryan reached down and stroked himself. Any remaining control I had vanished.

His other hand gripped the small of my back and pulled me onto his lap like we'd done before, but this time felt entirely different. There were no shorts between my butt and his cock. He pressed against me, and I felt how much he wanted to be inside me. He pulsed and twitched. I ground against him, and he pushed me down.

"Do you have any lube?"

I couldn't stop the laugh. "At my office? Uh, that would be no."

He chuckled. "Guess we'll have to do this the old-fashioned way."

I cocked my head, having absolutely no idea what he meant—until he spat on his palm.

"You're not serious, are you?"

He moistened his cock beneath me, never losing eye contact—and never answering.

He filled his palm again. I watched in fascination, unsure if this was still a good idea.

This time, his fingers traced my hole, slickening it, brushing against its opening with only the slightest pressure. I flinched, then shivered again. The tip of a finger slipped inside, and he swirled it slowly around. Another shudder ran through me, and I squeezed his shoulders.

He pulled his finger out, wet it again, then returned it. This time deeper.

I felt his knuckle. Then it slipped past. He retreated, then pressed in once more. In and out as my hole began to trust his touch.

When a second finger snuck in, I clinched.

"Easy, baby. Just relax." He wet his hand again, then two fingers broached the entrance as he kissed my chest. I shut my eyes and let my head fall back. His kisses and fingers pressed and probed, no longer gentle, now insistent with need and desire. I found myself levering up and down, urging his fingers onward, inward.

He pulled them out, and I heard him wet his hand again. I dared not look.

This time, fingers didn't return to my hole. His dripping cock pressed against my rim, soft and stiff at the same time. I thought I felt more than spittle, a slickness no water could provide. I reached back, thrilled to feel the oily smoothness of pre-cum, and pressed down, but he held me up, teasing my desire with his, taunting my hole with his hardness.

Then he pressed himself into me.

"Owwww!"

God, that hurt.

He pulled back. "Are you okay?"

"Don't you dare pull out. Just go slow. Give me a minute. You're ramming a Mac truck up my ass."

He laughed. "You're *so* romantic."

"Just shut up and fuck me."

"Now who's bossy?" He grinned.

Without warning, he slid all the way into me. The weight of my body straddling him pressed his cock so deep he hit some inner wall to a chamber I never knew existed. I groaned as the pain became wrapped in ecstasy. My back arched.

He stilled, wrapped his arms around me, and held me tight.

I looked down, confused.

"Don't move. Just let me be inside you."

One hand gripped my back while the other cupped my cheek.

We didn't grind or screw or fuck. There wasn't even another thrust.

We simply sat—joined as one person—and kissed.

21

THREE-WAY CALLING

"So neither of you *finished*?" Dwayne asked.

I described our lunch, then the office tour, without leaving out a single detail. The passion I'd felt in that moment poured out of me. Smitten no longer described what I felt for Ryan. I was seriously falling for this one. Connie was on the three-way call again, and my sheltered PK sensibilities were embarrassed by the explicit discussion of our escapade. Yes, she and I shared everything, and had talked about more butts, boobs, and wieners than I could count, but something about sharing my own private experience turned me into an awkward teenager.

"Well, no. He said he wanted to save that, that he only wanted to be with me in that moment as one person."

Connie sighed loudly into the receiver. "That's the most romantic thing I've ever heard."

Dwayne snorted.

"I thought so too," I said. "The kissing was incredible, especially while he was, you know, *up there*."

Connie giggled.

"After all this time, you still turn bashful just talking about sex. We have so much work to do, Connie," Dwayne said.

She giggled again. "I don't know. Our little chick seems to be growing new feathers every day."

"Uh, you two know I'm on the phone, right?"

That drew another round of amusement from the peanut gallery.

"I still can't believe you did that *in your office*. How will you ever sit in that chair and not think about that day?"

Huh. I hadn't thought about that. Now she'd planted a seed.

Dammit.

"Yeah, you'll be sitting there crunching numbers or working on some spreadsheet and your butt will tingle every time the leather squeaks." Dwayne was loving this conversation.

"Ha ha. Very funny. I'm a professional. I can handle it."

He snorted. "Professional who just bonked his boyfriend in his office chair."

"He's not my boyfriend. At least, I don't think he is yet. We haven't talked about it." We'd been dating for nearly two months, having lunch most Saturdays and Sundays, chatting online or on the phone several times each day. Did that make us boyfriends?

"So, how did you leave things?" Connie asked.

My mood sobered. "That's more the part I wanted to ask you two about. It was weird. There we were, peg-in-hole in my office chair, and his watch chimed. He looked down and got this look on his face. It wasn't fear, but it was *something*. He looked back up and gently pulled us apart, then told me he had somewhere to be and needed to go. It was all so…I don't know. Abrupt."

"Did he tell you where he was going?" Connie asked.

"No, just that he had somewhere to be. Even the way he phrased it made my hair stand on end."

Dwayne grunted. "I'm not sure you'd know what was standing on end in that moment, but we'll go with it. You've said things like this before about Ryan, how he won't do dinner during the week and logs off chats a little too quickly sometimes. As much as I like to tease you, your gut is solid. You should trust it."

"What does that mean? What are you saying?"

Dwayne's breath came in rasps down the phone line as he thought. "You know Ryan. We don't. From everything you've told us, he's a great guy worth getting to know. Just be cautious. You've sensed red flags; they could be nothing, but they could be something. Keep your eyes open and guard that last bit of your heart you haven't given him yet."

"I haven't given—"

"Uh-huh. You have. Don't even try to deny it," Connie cut in. "And that's amazing, but Dwayne's right. If you smell something off, just step carefully."

22

THE GOLDEN GATE

When Ryan's monthly trek to home office called, he invited me to join him.

I was stunned. No one had ever invited me on a trip, certainly not across the country to the Holy Land o' Gays. I'd also never been to San Francisco, and he said he wanted to show me what his trips were like.

He said he'd racked up so many frequent flyer points from all his work trips that he'd never be able to spend them all. The whole trip, minus meals, would be paid for by vendors and points programs. He described a luxury hotel, elegant meals, black car service, and loads of free time to explore and play tourist. It sounded like a four-day Michael-spoiling-in-the-making.

Like the wise woman said in *Pretty Woman*, "We need a little sucking up over here."

After a few minutes of appropriate, "Oh, I can't accept that," being countered by, "Oh, but you can," my defenses crumbled, and I agreed to go. There was never a question, I was just being polite with the mock refusal—and he knew it. Sneaky bastard.

Two days later, the lovely people at American Airlines ushered us to our first-class seats and offered a complimentary glass of champagne. Was that normal on flights? Ryan grinned broadly as he took a flute from the flight attendant and passed it to me. I was already putty in his hands. Add alcohol and it was a merry flight indeed.

A black SUV pulled up to the curb as we exited the airport. LOWELL was printed in neat lettering on a sign in the window. I'd expected a car, but this decked-out SUV was pretty hot.

Ryan hadn't lied about the hotel. Holy crap, his company put him up in fancy digs. Our room was nosebleed high in a skyscraper, offering views of the city and bay I thought only came in postcards. I set my roller bag down and flopped onto the bed. It swallowed me up. Between the plush comforter and the heavenly mattress, I wasn't sure I'd ever want to move—until Ryan leapt on top of me and started tickling.

"If I pee everywhere, you'll have to get us a new room," I called out between gasps.

He howled with delight and pressed his evil digits harder into my ribs.

We wandered down to the lobby sports bar for lunch, then my guide took me on a walking tour of downtown. That was the first time I'd ever held hands with a guy while walking down crowded streets. My eyes darted from one passerby to the next, anticipating a snide remark or snarly look, but no one gave us a second glance.

When we returned to our room and the door clicked shut, Ryan grabbed me around the waist and tossed me onto the overstuffed chair in the corner. He wrapped his arms around me and kissed my neck. Between pecks, he rattled off our agenda for the week.

"We have to do the Golden Gate Bridge."

"Are we going to walk across it?" I asked.

"Nah. It's a really long walk, and that would kill too much of our time."

"Okay. What else?"

"Let's see, there's Chinatown, the Castro District, Alcatraz—"

"Alcatraz? As in *the* Alcatraz? The prison?"

He chuckled at my enthusiasm. "Yep. It's been closed as a jail for years, but they do tours. Better be good or I'll lock you up."

"What if I want to be locked up with you?" My eyes were suddenly sparkling with mischief. "Maybe we need to check out the showers so I can drop the soap. I hear that leads to interesting encounters in prison."

"You're bad." He kissed my neck again. "Besides, if you want to drop the soap, there's nowhere around with a more comfortable shower than this room."

"Mr. Lowell, are you propositioning me?"

He grinned. "I'll knock the soap out of your hand if I have to. You're mine this week."

I craned my neck to nibble his earlobe. "Yes, sir. Anything you want, sir. I'm all yours, sir."

"Finally, he shows me proper respect. This may be a great trip, after all."

That earned him a playful punch on the arm.

RYAN TOOK THE NEXT DAY OFF, AND WE HIT THE aforementioned tourist destinations. As promised, the views from the Golden Gate Bridge were stunning. I'd never realized how wide San Fran's bay was. A tourist marker we passed estimated the bay's total surface area at sixteen hundred square miles. The ever-present breeze kept whitecapped water churning in every direction.

The Castro was eye-opening. Rainbow flags fluttered everywhere. Even the sidewalks shed their monotone in favor of festive colors. Bookstores, of both the peep and literary variety, sat shoulder to shoulder with restaurants, gift shops, bars…you name it.

Then there were the open displays of affection. Hell, that's gentle. Guys were practically naked and doing it on the street. Other than the one homeless man peeing on the sidewalk, I didn't see anyone *actually* naked, but they were darn close, and I got the feeling that all bets were off after dark. San Fran just had that vibe. It was thrilling and terrifying at the same time.

I felt like a newborn gay with wide eyes and jaw agape.

Chinatown turned out to be my favorite area. I'd always had a fascination with all things Asian, and this neighborhood did not disappoint. Shop after shop offered foods I couldn't identify, and antiques dating back to periods in Chinese history I'd read about in college classes years earlier. It felt like walking back in time.

I met a group of Buddhist priests strolling from their temple to a local restaurant. They gave me a primer on Chinatown's history, and suggested the best shops and restaurants that most tourists would never notice. Before we parted ways, one of the priests reached into a pocket of his robe and pulled out two coins with centers that had been hollowed out in a square. Faded Chinese characters were embossed in the bronze metal.

"Take these to remember us." He pointed to one of the symbols. "This is Kangxi. He was emperor during the Qing dynasty in the seventeenth century. I feel his spirit in you."

I stared at the coins in my hand. "I can't take these. They're so old. Aren't they valuable?"

He chuckled. "Everything is old in China. These coins are common. Take them. I hope they bring you luck."

I thanked him and we said our goodbyes. I didn't understand how coins could bring luck or how Kangxi might be lurking in my spirit, but it was the coolest souvenir I could have hoped for.

Ryan had to work during the other days of the trip, so I wandered around town and enjoyed exploring more of Chinatown's shops. Most nights we ordered room service and watched movies on the wall-sized flat-screen.

On Valentine's Day, we fed each other chocolate-covered strawberries and sipped champagne. Ryan insisted the first sip occur while our arms were interlocked. We proved just how uncoordinated we both were with that maneuver, laughing like schoolboys the whole time.

It was one of the most romantic weeks I'd ever experienced.

23

SHOCK AND AWE

Ryan and I were supposed to have lunch the next day. As I was getting dressed, the phone rang.

"Hey." Ryan's voice sounded strange.

"Hey you. Everything okay? Still on for lunch?"

He didn't say anything for a long moment. When he spoke, it was clear he'd been crying. "I don't want to lose you."

What the hell?

"Ryan, what's going on? Talk to me."

"You might, when I tell you…"

I waited while he gathered himself.

"Michael, I'm married."

My mind couldn't register what he'd said. All my circuits overloaded at the same time. I couldn't move, couldn't breathe. Words wouldn't form.

"You're…what?"

"I'm married. Her name is Diane. We've been married for eighteen years."

I don't remember sitting on the couch or turning the TV off.

"We have two children. An eight-year-old boy and a five-year-old girl."

I wanted him to stop talking, to stop telling me all this. We were supposed to go to lunch. We were supposed to be falling in love. He was supposed to be…so much.

The walls of my apartment began to close in, and I wiped tears from my cheek.

"I'm so sorry I didn't tell you. I never thought I'd meet a guy who…made me feel like this. I thought it was all just fun, that it didn't mean anything, like experimenting."

Anger bubbled up. "You thought we were an *experiment?*"

"No, of course not. I mean, at first, but not now." He blew out his exasperation. "Michael, I've fallen in love with you. That wasn't supposed to happen—with anyone. I didn't mean for it to happen. Now all I can think about is being with you."

"But you're married—*with kids*. How do you think that could work?"

"I don't know. All I know is I don't want to be without you."

What was I supposed to say to that? I wanted to be with him more than anything, but the Ryan I was falling in love with wasn't the man I thought I was getting to know. The *real* Ryan had been married for *nearly twenty years* and had two kids. What was he doing online, meeting guys, dating? Did he have so little respect for his wife and the promise he'd made to her? How could he betray his family like that? Now he talked about us like we were a couple, like we had a future. How could I ever trust him? If he'd play around on his wife and kids, would he respect any promise he made to me? Did his promises mean anything?

And then my father's voice echoed in my head with one word.

Adultery.

I'd had sex with a *married man*. That violated so much of what I believed, what I was taught. Set aside the whole gay thing, we'd trampled all over something I'd always held as precious: a marriage between two loving people.

My anger morphed into misery, then frustration, then guilt.

Always guilt.

My mind was spinning so fast I'd nearly forgotten

the receiver was still pressed to my ear. Then he spoke again.

"I get it if you don't ever want to see me again." There was such pain in his voice. It broke my heart. I wanted—no, I *needed*—to comfort him.

"Ryan, that's not what I want, but…" I struggled to form a coherent thought. "I don't know how I feel or what to think. I need some time."

"That's fine," he responded quickly. "Take all the time you need. I'm here."

"Okay. Yeah, I know. Thanks."

I ran out of words and hung up the receiver.

24

WHIPLASH

I sat across the table from Connie in the seat Ryan was supposed to fill. She ate her chicken and veggies, quietly observing me push Brussels around my plate without ever tasting one. Roasters was one of my favorite comfort-food places in town, but my appetite had disappeared faster than my trust in Ryan.

"This sucks," I said, unable to meet her eyes.

"Yeah. It does."

I slumped back in my chair and continued playing with my food.

After several minutes, she broke the silence. "Are you going to see him again?"

I looked up. "How can I? He's *married*. I've abandoned a lot of what I believed growing up, but I've never lost my faith in a promise. Marriage, religiously blessed or not, is a sacred oath. We pretty much shattered his last weekend."

"I'm pretty sure he shattered it before he met you."

I folded my arms. "What do you mean?"

"You don't think you're his first, do you? He knew his way around your body and mouth like he'd been there before. At least, that's how it sounded when you described your little office visit." She cracked the slightest smile to lighten the mood.

My frown didn't budge. "Yeah. He knew what he was doing. That doesn't make my part in breaking his word any better. I feel terrible for his wife—and kids. He has two kids. What would they think if they knew their dad was running around on their mother with men?"

"Probably no worse than if he cheated with women."

I gave her a solid eye roll.

"Okay, we are in the South. You're right," she admitted.

"What am I going to do, Connie? I know I should just tell him I can't see him anymore, but—" My voice caught in my throat.

"You've fallen in love with him, haven't you?"

I looked up with watery eyes and nodded.

"Oh, sweet pea."

The server appeared and asked if something was wrong with my uneaten food. Connie saved me from trying to speak. "He's just not feeling well. Can we have a to-go box?"

The server gave me a sympathetic look, nodded back to Connie, and strode away.

She leaned forward and took my hand. "Look at me."

My head rose slowly.

"You don't have to make any decisions right now. You just learned about this. Give yourself a day or two to let everything sink in, to figure out what you really feel."

"How will a couple days change the ring on his finger?" I asked. "Oh, wait. He didn't wear one. That was all part of the deception."

The more I talked, the angrier I got. Ryan had not just cheated on his family, he'd also lied to me, over and over. His profile lied. His words about feelings for me lied. Even his empty ring finger lied.

Had he ever been truthful?

I seethed as the server brought the check. Connie handled things, probably fearing the eruption she sensed was coming. If there was ever an empath in this world, it was Connie. She could feel a twitch across a room and know how everyone was feeling. Like her memory, it was creepy.

"Listen to me. Everything you're feeling right now is normal. I'd be worried about you if you weren't bundled up with anger and hurt, maybe with a decent serve of guilt thrown in. You're good at that one. Just don't be too hard on yourself—or Ryan—until you know the whole story. If he's the guy you thought he was yesterday, he deserves that much. You deserve it too."

I glared at her, then my gaze softened. She was right. Ryan might be a lying cheater, but I knew he was a good man, a great guy. Shit, that even sounded terrible in my head. Why did this have to be so hard? Why couldn't I just meet someone like Ryan, fall madly in love, and never have to worry about dating or cheaters—or anything—ever again? The longer I sat and stared at the rugged wooden tabletop, the more confused, angry, sad—and guilty—I became. I hadn't even noticed Connie stand. She'd been waiting for me to get up for a couple minutes.

"Up. You can sulk at home."

I finally cracked a hint of a smile. "Yes, Mom."

She slapped my shoulder playfully as I stood. "I'll take ma'am, but I ain't yo mama."

She giggled, and my smile broadened. God, I loved her.

I LEFT LUNCH AND DROVE TO THE GYM. MY HEART wasn't into working out, but I hoped the rush of a good body pump might lift my mood. It usually did.

The gym wasn't very busy, but there were always a few hotties strutting around. Most took their work-outs seriously, but some clearly viewed the gym as more social than physical. The preeners were in full force that day.

Ten minutes into my treadmill warm-up, I mashed the *stop* button and dragged my sorry ass home. I was on the verge of tears. No amount of endorphins could wash them away.

When I got home, I logged into AOL and Ryan was waiting on my friends list. He IMed me imme-diately.

HEY.

I logged out as fast as I could.

Yeah, I was a wuss. Avoiding him like that was probably childish, but I wasn't ready to face him. The jumble of emotions in my gut were doing their impression of a Wide World of Wrestling bout, and I couldn't figure out how to end the round. The last thing I wanted was for him to ask how I was doing— or say he wanted to see me again.

My conscience, with its smoothly filed corners that barely registered any pain these days, found ways to prick my heart at the thought of dating a married man, even one as amazing as Ryan. I wanted to find some way to justify everything, but the moral compass instilled in me years ago wouldn't allow it. I doubted even my little devil would tread on that ground.

Then the phone rang.

I figured it was Dwayne. Enough time had passed since lunch for Connie to call in backup. She'd never seen me like this, and I felt sure she'd loop Dwayne in before I had the chance. I grabbed the receiver and pulled the scrunchy cord over the couch.

"Hello?"

"Hey."

It was Ryan.

My throat became suddenly dry. My heart turned into an Olympic sprinter. I opened my mouth to say something—I had no idea what—but Ryan spoke first.

"I told her."

What? Who was *her*? And what did he tell her? He sounded miserable, but there was a twinge of something else in his voice I couldn't identify. Hope? Fear? I wasn't sure.

"She didn't throw anything, but there was a lot of yelling. She told me to leave."

My heart begged to reach out and hold him.

"Ryan, what are you saying? I'm not following."

There was a long pause.

"I told Diane I'm…gay. She asked if I'd acted on it, so I told her about hooking up with guys when I was on business trips, and a few times here."

Oh shit.

"I told her I'd been doing that once a month or so for the last five or six years. I can't blame her for screaming or being upset. I get it. What I did was terrible—for both of us."

I barely knew what to say. Ryan started crying.

"Why?" My voice croaked out in a whisper. "Why did you tell her?"

It took him another minute to stop crying. As long as I live, I'll never forget the words he spoke next.

"Because I'm in love with you."

I didn't think my heart could beat any faster, but it did. What I couldn't tell was whether that was from fear or anger—or the thrill of being told the man I'd fallen for was also in love with me. I wanted to scream at him for lying and deceiving me, for cheating on his wife, but my heart craved falling into his arms and sharing his warmth again.

An overwhelming sense of guilt doused that ember before it could spark. What kind of guy has such mixed emotions about betrayal? Who was I turning into? I wasn't sure I liked the answer that echoed in my head.

"Michael, please say something."

How long had I been silent? I could barely think.

"I'm in love with you too," slipped out.

What the literal fuck had I just said? The receiver dropped into my lap as my hand flew over my mouth.

I tried to grab the words and shove them back down, but they'd flown into the phone and refused to return. I knew it was true, that I *was* falling for him, but given everything, it was the *last* thing I should've said. I was supposed to be walking away, standing up for my principles, refusing to take part in his lie.

Was it still a lie?

He'd come clean. Sure, he'd broken their vows— and a few Georgia laws— but he wasn't *lying* to Diane anymore.

I heard him release the breath he'd been holding. "Really? Seriously? Even after—"

"Yeah, seriously." Shit, I was sinking fast. Why did I just confirm the thing I shouldn't have said in the first place?

Fuck. Fuck. Fuck.

I had to fix this. "I still don't know how I feel about everything, though. You're married with kids— and you never told me any of it. You weren't just lying to her. You were lying to *me* the whole time too."

"I know." His voice was so small, so riddled with pain. "I'm so sorry. I didn't want to, but I didn't know what to do. The more we got to know each other, the more I knew my life was about to change, and I couldn't figure out how to navigate between the two lives I was living."

Shit. That would be hard.

Growing up, I didn't know I was gay, didn't have a clue. Given the right planets lining up, I could just have easily been Ryan, married with kids and struggling with my true feelings. My heart shifted again.

"How have you lived like this for so long?"

"It was easy at first. Diane really is great. We were happy, and I thought my attraction to guys would just go away once we got married and had kids."

"Did it? Go away, I mean?"

"I guess—for a while. Maybe I was just so distracted with life to pay attention. Looking back, there were men at the gym, or at work, really handsome guys. They caught my eye in a way that was different, but nothing I understood. I never acted on anything."

"When did that change?"

He thought a moment. "We had Alan, and everything was amazing. Diane bounced back from that pregnancy like a champ. He grew so fast. There really wasn't time for anything other than taking care of the house and chasing his squirmy butt."

I could hear the smile in his voice as he recalled happier times. Then it sobered again.

"When we had Elaine, a lot changed. That pregnancy was really hard on Diane. After Elaine was born, Diane was bedridden for weeks, and couldn't do very much for months. Alan was a toddler. That didn't help. When my company insisted I start visiting home office twice each month for a week, Diane took the brunt of everything, taking care of the kids while still not feeling one hundred percent. I felt terrible for what she went through, but didn't know how to help.

"When she'd finally recovered…I don't know… we were different; distant. Everything felt like we were just going through the motions, doing everything we needed to do, but neither of us was happy to be doing it. We went to counseling, talked to friends, went on vacations together. We really tried. Nothing seemed to help. We didn't mean to drift. We just did."

He was silent for a time. Then his voice crept out, quiet and strained.

"Five years ago, almost to the month, I was in San Fran on one of those trips. It had been a long day, and I got back to my hotel late. I was starving and exhausted, so I headed downstairs to the hotel bar.

While I was waiting for my dinner, this guy in shorts and a T-shirt walked in. He'd just finished a workout in the hotel gym, and he was sweaty. His shirt stuck to his body in all the right ways. I didn't mean to stare. My eyes just wouldn't look away. Neither did his.

"He was my first."

25

BENDS AND FORKS

Ryan and I talked for over an hour.

He told me more of his journey, how the random first encounter in San Francisco bloomed into other encounters. Then he discovered AOL, and finding occasional companions on his travels became easier. He said he only hooked up a couple times a year, but my gut told me it happened more often. My heart ached as he fought tears and talked about Diane and the kids. While he'd continued to explore his sexuality, his relationship with them—especially with Diane—weighed heavily on his conscience.

From the anguish in his voice, I could tell it was crushing him—and had been for years.

My uptight PK brain wanted to be offended, to be angry and stand up for Diane. He *had* broken his vows, repeatedly. He *had* lied for years, hidden his truth from her—and himself. I understood the journey, the battle of identity that tore your soul apart, and empathized with his searching and questioning. Hell, I'd followed a similar path; virtually every gay person does. The self-doubt and self-loathing were familiar, like a second skin I'd learned to shed when necessary. Eventually, we grew past those scars—at least, that's what I hoped would happen. Mine still felt fresh some days. I'm sure his were raw and painful.

But I hadn't committed my life to someone else or fathered children who depended on my guidance and faithfulness. His discovery of himself would shatter their world. It would forever alter the trajectory of their lives. Alan was old enough to understand, but Elaine wouldn't. All she would know was the loss of a father she loved.

My heart ached for those little ones.

It was hours later, and I'd thought of nothing else since our phone call ended. I hadn't eaten; I had barely moved. Every time I thought I'd reached a conclusion, my head would argue the other side.

As quickly as I steeled myself to be righteous, I remembered how it felt to just talk with Ryan. There was a freedom, an openness, a fluidity to our conversations. That was something I'd never experienced with anyone, not even Connie or Dwayne. I'd never thought of conversation as an intimate act, but even our first date—the one I didn't think was that special —was filled with hours of intimacy through words and the simplicity of being together.

Sure, Ryan was hot as fuck. I now knew his fuck was hot too, but that wasn't what flooded my mind as I considered walking away. It was our chats. It was lunch at Cowtippers or breakfast at Le Peep. It was watching him get sugar packets dumped in his lap, and the way his poochy lip would try to curl but fail.

His eyes never failed. They smiled as wide as any mouth. They positively glowed when he was happy.

I would miss all that. I didn't just crave that level of closeness; I *needed* it.

What was I supposed to do now? Could I stay with him given what he was doing to his family, what he'd already done? Could I trust he wouldn't do that to me?

Was that even a fair question?

He was facing his sexual identity. It was probably the first time he'd been fully honest with himself in four decades of life. Despite all the lying, he was actually seeking an honest answer.

The irony of that made me pause.

In the silence of my tortured thoughts, the phone rang. It was Dwaync.

"Just checking in. How did lunch go?"

Shit. I have to go through this all over again, I thought.

"Hang on. Let me get Connie on the line. I'd rather not have to repeat the whole show."

"That doesn't sound good," he said as I clicked the three-way call button.

"Hi, sweet pea." Connie's singsong warmed me through the receiver.

"Sweet pea?" Dwayne barked a laugh.

Connie went in mama lion mode. "It's my nickname for the sweetest pea in Atlanta. Don't you dare make fun of it."

"Easy, tiger. I'll call him pea from now on."

I gave them a halfhearted laugh. "Very funny, you two. Connie, would you mind giving Dwayne the *Reader's Digest* version of today? I don't think I can go over it again."

"Aww. You really are down, aren't you?" she said sympathetically. "Bottom line: Ryan's married with two kids. He's been playing around on the side while on business trips. He told Ryan all this, then—without warning—told his wife. She kicked him out. Now Ryan is homeless and sad, and Michael is miserable and confused about what he should do."

"Well, shit." Dwayne was never short for words, and he rarely cursed. This was bad.

"Can you give me a little more than that? I need my sherpa today, more than ever. Give me pearls of wisdom."

He grunted a laugh. "I'm not sure how wise I can be in this situation. What do you want advice on?"

That was frustrating. Wasn't it obvious?

"Ryan cheated and lied—*for years*. He's breaking up a wonderful family. I need to tell him to take a hike, right? The last thing I should do is date a liar and cheat, a wounded man who's just now finding himself. Right?"

Connie kept quiet, and Dwayne took forever to respond. By the time he spoke, I was off the couch and pacing.

"Do you love him?"

Fuck. That wasn't an answer, and it definitely wasn't on my list of things I thought he'd ask. I wasn't even sure I knew the answer.

"Maybe. I think so. I don't know. I'm falling in love with him. Is that the same thing?"

"Yeah, it counts." Dwayne's deep sigh blew through the phone line. "Look, Michael, I know you want this to be black and white, for there to be a *right* answer. That's how you were raised, to follow the one true path. Unfortunately, life isn't that clean and neat. Most paths bob and weave, probably fork a hundred times, and they're rarely free of obstacles or debris."

"I'm not following. Are you comparing Ryan's cheating to a bend in the road?"

"Don't get impatient. Hang with me." He had steel

in his voice I'd never heard before. I recognized it as the steel of a father teaching his son. I'd never loved Dwayne more than I did in that moment.

"You should know better than anyone what it feels like to come out later in life. You grew up thinking you were straight. Hell, the night we met, you practically preached a sermon about it. I seem to recall us sitting in a gay bar while you did that, but whatever."

Connie snorted.

"My point is this: if Ryan's family is anything like yours, he was taught, from the time he could understand, that his job in life was to grow up, get married, have a family, and carry the family name into the future. Based on what you've told us about him, he never questioned that. He did as he was raised to do. He got married. He had kids. Somewhere along the way, like you, his true nature found the surface and demanded to be acknowledged. While his actions were his own, and I understand how you would see them as cheating, it sounds like he felt trapped in a life that didn't fit. It might've been a good life, but was it truly the one meant for him? I actually feel sorry for him."

For the second time that day, a conversation held so many conundrums that my head hurt. My pacing was furious. I wanted to throw the phone. "That doesn't help me know what I should do."

Dwayne switched to a soft tone. "I can't give you the answer. It has to be yours."

With those words, my heart sank even lower. I hadn't thought that was possible.

How was I supposed to come up with the answers? My heart was in my throat and pounding. I wanted to cry, but tears wouldn't even cooperate. Now the two people I knew could guide me through this mess—

"Let me ask you this," Dwayne said. "Based on your conversation today, how does Ryan feel about all this?"

I didn't have to think about that one. "He's miserable. He knows he just shattered a family he's spent two decades building, and that damage will continue for the rest of his life—of all their lives. I can't tell whether he's more angry with himself or guilty. If I didn't know how much he loves his kids, I'd be worried about him hurting himself."

"What about how he feels toward Diane now?" Dwayne asked.

"He talked about her a lot today, told me how they met, the early part of their lives together. He loves her, and that's making this so much harder. He said the hurt in her eyes when she kicked him out felt like a sword in his gut. He said they'd never really had a fight in all those years—and then this happened."

No one spoke for another painful moment as I replayed our conversation in my mind.

"He said he knows she'll come around and accept him for who he is, that she's hurt and feels betrayed. He broke down crying several times as he talked about what his confession had done to her."

"That actually makes me feel better about his situation," Dwayne said.

"Huh? How?" I asked.

"If he didn't feel that guilt or understand clearly what his actions were doing to his family, he'd be a lot worse than a liar and cheat in my book. Nothing will ever make up for the damage he's causing right now, but I can at least understand him. He doesn't sound like one of those guys to just walk away from his obligations, especially those he loves."

"No, he's not like that. He'll never turn his back on Diane and the kids."

Where was Dwayne going with all this? The last thing I wanted to do was rationalize away the gravity of Ryan's actions. He might make my skin tingle, but I dreamed of a lot more in a relationship than just a hot body by my side. I wanted a guy with character and the strength to back it up, even when things were hard —*especially* when things were hard.

Then it hit me. That's exactly what Dwayne was getting at. Could Ryan honestly be expected to live a lie for the rest of his life? That's what his marriage to a woman was. He knew he was gay, especially after all the years of experimentation. Was a man in that position expected to live with a commitment he'd made before he truly knew himself? What kind of tortured, lonely life would that be?

The stubborn, conservative PK in me answered harshly. *Yes, absolutely, he should've lived with his decision and suffered like the sinner he was.*

God, hearing my own voice, how I would've answered a few years ago, I cringed. Had I really been that cruel; possessed so little compassion? Weren't religions supposed to uplift people, especially those hurting or in need? Had I only learned the part of the Good Book that condemned?

In that moment, I hated who I'd become—or who I had been. I wasn't sure. Everything was so confusing.

"Michael." Connie's voice cut in.

"Yeah?" I croaked.

"If you love him, don't give up. If you leave now, you'll never be able to go back. Everything you've told me about Ryan makes me think he's special. Most people never get a shot at that. There's always time to walk away later if you think that's the right thing."

"Just keep your eyes open and take it slow, alright?" Dwayne cautioned.

"So…you're saying I *should* stay with him?"

"I'm saying we won't judge you—or him—if you do. He'll have to face what he's done. Like you said, he'll be facing it for the rest of his life with his family. What *you* do with him in his next chapter has yet to be written. You have an opportunity to find out what those pages hold—*together*."

Did Connie really want me to give him a chance?

My heart lifted for the first time all day.

I still wasn't sure how my conscience would react tomorrow, but I *was* falling in love with him, and Dwayne was right. He'd never had a chance to know himself, to find himself—whatever that meant. Maybe I was put in his life to help him do that.

Or maybe I was justifying what *I* wanted.

Dammit. Why does life suck so hard sometimes?

"Thanks, guys. I love you both so much."

"We love you too, sweet pea." Connie sounded chipper again.

"Yeah, sweet pea. Me too." Sarcasm dripped from Dwayne's voice, but it was full of warmth too.

We hung up, and I flopped back onto the couch and stared at the ceiling. My heart might've settled, but my stomach was still doing somersaults. There wouldn't be much sleep tonight.

26

A NEW BEGINNING

Ryan and I sat across the same table we'd sat at when we first met. Caribou was special to us. The irony of returning here for this conversation wasn't lost on me as I looked into his deep, troubled eyes.

A week had passed. Ryan and I had chatted every day online, but had only spoken once over the phone. The strain in his voice on that call broke my heart.

As I cradled a coffee mug in my hands, he spoke quietly about the conversations he'd had with Diane, and the couple times he'd gone to see the kids. They had asked a thousand questions, all the ones you'd expect confused and frightened children to ask in their situation. Ryan's voice trembled.

I'll never know how he got through that first week —or how they did.

The bedrock of his emotional stability, his family, had been irrevocably altered—possibly shattered—and there was no way of knowing if he would forge relationships built on new truths or lose them entirely.

His watery eyes told me he had resigned himself to losing me as well.

I couldn't take the anguish on his face anymore, so I reached out and gripped his hands in mine.

His eyes widened.

I'd had a speech planned, but every word of it fled when my mouth opened. What came out was a stream of consciousness driven from somewhere deep inside, and I couldn't stop it.

"Ryan, I've thought about you a lot this week. Shit, you're all I've thought about." I was fumbling, but had to press forward. "I can't understand what you felt when you married Diane, or how your loyalties were strained as you realized your true nature. A huge part of me struggles with your vows, and the commitment you made to your kids, and how all that will change going forward—but just as I ask you to be honest with yourself, I have to do the same."

He was holding his breath.

"I'm in love with you."

There, I said it. Fuck, what now?

I blundered on. "I've tried to walk away from you. I've done it a million times in my mind, but every time you return. Ryan, I can't imagine my life without you in it. I know we just met a few months ago, and that sounds totally crazy, but it's the truth. It's my truth."

The death grip he put on my hands told me all I needed to know. Then he spoke.

"I'm so in love with you it hurts," he said. "When I'm not obsessing over how I hurt Diane or what will happen with the kids, I'm missing you. All I want is to be with you, to talk with you, to feel safe next to you. I've never felt that with anyone."

I made him feel safe? This man, twelve years older, who ran a massive business and was more confident and surer of himself than anyone I'd ever known, found shelter in *my* arms?

A tear escaped his eye. I reached up and wiped it with my thumb. He leaned into my touch.

"I want that too," I whispered. "More than anything."

We'd run out of words, so we sat clutching each other's hands on the table, our eyes never leaving the other's. Lord knows what the people in that coffee shop must've thought about the two gays holding hands and crying in the corner. For the first time in my life, I didn't care.

"So what do we do now?" I asked.

The happier version of the man sitting before me

peeked out. "I don't know about you, but being miserable makes me hungry. Can we go to Le Peep and get stuff thrown at us?"

I grinned. "That sounds perfect."

BETTY GREETED US AT THE DOOR. SHE GAVE RYAN AN odd look, apparently having some diner-waitress-Spidey-sense that picked up on the mood of our day, then led us to a lonely table in the corner of the restaurant.

As we sat, she pointed an accusing order pad at Ryan. "Honey, you look terrible—and you're too cute to look terrible. What's going on?"

Ryan shrugged and gave her a weak smile. "Rough week. We're okay, though."

He glanced sideways at me when he said "we." I couldn't stop the warmth that swelled within.

Betty missed nothing. "Yeah, you two are bookends, alright. Best matched set I've seen in a while."

Ryan turned to me, and I melted into an inarticulate, babbling mess of rainbow glitter. "Yeah, he's dreamy. I mean, we're dreamy. No. We're good. I mean great. Matched. You said matched set. That's perfect. Oh, never mind."

Ryan grinned. "What he said."

She barked a laugh and waved her pad. "Told ya. Now, what's for breakfast?"

We ordered our usual. Ryan got eggs Benedict, and I ordered wholegrain pancakes with bacon and over-medium eggs. Le Peep had the fancy flavored creamers on the table, and our hands were a jumbled blur as we raced to grab the last of the hazelnut. There was a normalcy to ordering breakfast, something soothing I didn't fully understand. We both needed it.

"Where did you leave things with Diane?" I'd wanted to focus on lighter subjects, but needed some idea of what the future held.

He sighed as he stirred his coffee. "She wants me moved out by the end of the month. Guess it's time to find a place of my own."

"You could stay with me," I blurted out.

Where the hell had that come from?

In all my ruminations, that idea had never crossed my mind. Dwayne and Connie were going to shit a brick. Don't get me wrong, the idea of waking up beside Ryan every day made my heart skip a beat, but it was far too soon for that step. My rational brain scolded me as soon as the words flew out of my mouth.

He looked up from his mug and quirked a brow. "Really?"

I was in it deep now. *Shit.*

I nodded. "Sure. My place isn't fancy. I don't even have end tables in the den, just cardboard moving boxes, but you can stay at my place as long as you need."

"It couldn't be long term. Diane would lose her mind if she knew I was living in your apartment."

I shot upright. "She knows about *me*?"

He nodded slowly. "I promised to tell her the whole truth, no more lies. She, uh, thinks you *turned* me."

I coughed. "Turned you? What am I, a vampire?"

"Something like that. 'Blood-sucking evil bastard' is probably closer to her description. You're the guy who stole my heart away from her." He raised his mug in salute. "It's not about you, really. She doesn't even know you. But she's looking for someone to blame, some explanation to ease the feeling that she failed, and you're the easy target."

"Wow." I leaned back. "I guess that makes sense. She knows she didn't do anything wrong, doesn't she? God, she can't carry guilt along with everything else. That's our job."

"Guilt is probably one of a hundred emotions she's feeling. And yes, I told her she's not to blame. It'll take time for her to understand that."

"Until then, I'm public enemy number one."

"Yeah, I'm pretty sure you won't be invited to Thanksgiving."

I knew he was trying to lighten the mood, but I couldn't pry myself out from the pile of shit he'd just dumped on me to acknowledge his attempt.

"I'll still need to find my own place." His eyes drifted back to his mug as he spoke his next words. "Maybe you could help me look?"

Was he asking me to help him find *his* new home, or a place for *us*? My brain danced between disbelief, elation, and complete shock. Was this even something I *should* consider? I mean, I had just asked him to move into my apartment. That was basically the same thing, just with cheaper furniture. Wasn't it?

He saw my mind whirling and grinned. "House shopping is more fun with somebody. Besides, it'll be fun to compare notes on what we both like and don't like. You know, for if we get a place together one day."

Guess that answered that.

My shoulders slumped. Why was I so disappointed? It was insane to even consider moving in together right now. He wasn't even divorced yet. Holy cow, had I shoved my head all the way up—

"Where'd you go?" He saved me from a terrible mental image.

"Sorry, house shopping sounds fun. Where were you thinking?"

"I work out of my house most of the time, so that makes things a little easier. Being close enough to help with the kids is the only real consideration. Maybe start with the Roswell area?"

"That's near my office."

He grinned and nodded.

He knew that. No freakin' way. He'd factored that in. That sneaky—

"I thought it might be nice to grab lunch during workdays."

I lit up. "If you're lucky, there might even be some lunchtime dessert. We can't exactly do a repeat in my office during a workday, but if you lived close, I could use my lunchtime for more…athletic adventures."

"Acrobatic is more like it, based on how your legs bent over that chair."

We both froze as Betty's voice cut through. "And just what were Michael's legs doing?"

Ryan actually turned redder than I did. I didn't know that was possible.

Proud she'd thoroughly embarrassed us, Betty leaned over and planted her palms on the table. There was very little of her cleavage we couldn't see. Gravity is an unforgiving force. "When I was your age, I could bend my legs—"

"And, we're done with breakfast," Ryan said, saving us once again. "Thank you so much, Betty."

She cackled. "Why do you think I always wear hoop earrings? Gotta be prepared for anything."

She tossed the check at Ryan's chest and laughed all the way back to the kitchen.

AROUND EIGHT O'CLOCK, THE SUN WAS STARTING TO set, and Atlanta's skyline was framed in brilliant hues of orange and yellow.

I greeted Ryan as he stood outside my apartment door. He had a duffel bag slung over his shoulder and a sheepish look on his face. "Still willing to take in a stray?"

I chuckled, gripped his face with both hands, and pulled him toward me for a kiss. "Strays are kind of my thing, especially hot ones."

"You think I'm hot?" He grinned.

I rolled my eyes. "You're far too vain to ask me that. No one with abs on his toes has the right to ask that question."

He looked down at his flip-flopped feet and cocked his head. "Huh. Washboard pinkie. Never noticed that before."

I slapped him playfully. "Just get in here."

He eyed the sparseness of my apartment but had the good grace not to say anything.

"I know. It's pretty lame, but I haven't had time to furnish the place yet."

"It's…minimalist."

I laughed as we entered my bedroom, the only room with a full complement of furniture.

"No, it's *empty*, but thank you. Just drop your duffel over there in the corner. I've cleared a couple drawers in the dresser for you." I motioned to the 1950s dresser my mom gave me when I went to college. I think she'd used it when *she* went to college. It was functional, but not very fashionable. I'd never cared until Ryan showed up. Now I was embarrassed.

"You cleared drawers for me?" he asked from the doorway.

"Don't get all mushy. It's a practical thing. Your clothes will get all wrinkled if they stay in that bag."

He shook his head, grinning ear to ear.

I knelt to open the two bottom drawers. As I rose, Ryan's strong hands wrapped around me from behind and pulled me tight against his body. I could smell his salty-sweet musk; his breath was hot against my neck. I surrendered completely and leaned my full weight against him.

"The clothes can wait." His voice was raspy and full of hunger.

Warm lips pressed against my neck. I felt the gentle nibble of teeth on my ear, sending a jolt down my spine. I tried to turn to face him, but he held me fast.

"Oh no. You stay where you are."

I was powerless to resist.

His hands gripped my chest, caressing and kneading, then slid down my stomach. Gentle fingers traced the outline of my abs through the fabric of my shirt before sneaking under and uniting our flesh.

His hands were warm, almost hot. His fingers tickled the tiny hairs trailing down my stomach, and I squirmed. He squeezed his arms tighter, gripping my body against his, and I felt how hard he'd become as he throbbed and pulsed.

Damn, I could feel it through my shorts. He ground against me, growling in my ear with each twist and turn.

Now *I* was pulsing. I moaned again, and he growled louder.

His hands traveled up my shirt until his fingers gripped my nipples. He teased, circling the base then grazing the tips. They'd never been sensitive before, but fire lit within them at his touch. What was this man doing to me?

Without warning, he pinched them between his thumb and forefinger, and my whole body lurched. In his grip, there was nowhere to go, and the blissful pain of his grasp shook us both. I tried to cry out, to say it hurt, but no words came, just a guttural howl. He twisted his pincers as his tongue rimmed the outside of my ear.

My cry deepened.

His tongue vanished and teeth began nibbling up and down my neck. His hands descended until they pressed the waistband of my shorts. When they fell to the floor, I stepped out of them as Ryan's palm wrapped around my hardened dick. It spasmed at his touch.

"There are so many things I've wanted to do to you," he whispered in my ear.

"Uh-huh," was all I got out.

He lifted my arms above my head and ripped off my shirt. Again, I tried to turn, but he gripped my shoulders to hold me in place, facing away from him.

"You're being a very bad boy. Keep that up, and I might have to punish you."

Punish? Oh, God. Please punish me. Punish me into the eighteenth century.

That was my inner voice. "Yeah?" was what squeaked out.

His hands drifted down my arms to rest on my

hips. I heard him settle on his knees. He kissed the small of my back, then licked it tenderly. His tongue ventured lower, teasing my crack as it edged ever closer. When his hands left my hips and parted my cheeks, I stumbled forward. He laughed as he caught me.

"So jumpy," he said as he turned me to face the bed then shoved me face down onto it. A second later, my legs were spread wide and his face was buried in the fold of my buttocks. I tried to lie still, but every time his tongue edged my hole, I squirmed. I lost track of time—hell, I lost track of everything. I'd only had one guy do that to me, and Ryan's passion blew the other dude's effort out of the water.

He lifted my butt up to get a better angle. My dick slid against the bedspread with each thrust of his face. The friction was driving me crazy.

He finally came up for air.

I glanced over my shoulder, then turned and sat up facing him. He cupped my cheek tenderly and stared with the most intensely passionate gaze ever pointed my way. I looked down after a moment, suddenly awkward and unsure, but he lifted my chin, forcing our eyes to lock once again.

"Thank you," he said.

My brow furrowed. What had I done?

"I know what it meant for you to give me a chance

after…everything. I don't deserve your faith or trust, but I hope to earn it one day. You make me want—"

I leaned forward, grabbed his face, and pulled him into an unrepentant kiss. A salty tang dribbled into my mouth from the fresh tears he'd shed, and his body trembled. The change from overheated passion to tender vulnerability kicked my caretaking senses into overdrive. I wrapped my arms around him and pulled him into me, holding him as tightly as he'd held me before.

After several minutes, his trembling and tears ceased.

His hand drifted back to my head and stroked my hair as his eyes explored every curve of my face. In that moment, I saw a different man; no, not different, deeper layers of the man I already knew. His leathery shell had peeled away, and the frightened, exposed, hopeful little boy beneath begged for acceptance and forgiveness.

My heart lurched as I leaned forward and kissed him again. "We're in this together now. You'll never be alone."

Ryan's last wall crumbled. He buried his face in my chest and heaved again.

I don't remember how long we lay there. Time didn't matter. Nothing did, other than holding Ryan and making him feel loved. As sad as his tears were, my need to care for someone filled my heart with a joy I hadn't known in years. I was still amazed that this wonderful man wanted to be with me, wanted me to be the one holding him in his times of happiness or pain.

He finally stirred. I turned so my back was upright on the headboard, and he found his knees and straddled my legs. With one hand, he brushed fingers lightly across my chest until they found a nipple. This time, rather than teasing or rough, he caressed it as one might the most fragile glass.

"You're so beautiful," he said.

When I blushed and looked away, he leaned down and kissed me deeply.

"I'm in love with you, Michael Reed."

His mouth stopped any reply. A heartbeat later, his tongue was caressing mine with the same gentleness it had my nipple. I think that sensation, more than any other, sent my heart and mind spinning.

As we kissed, I reached down and pulled the bottom of his shirt upward. With a toss, we'd moved on to his jeans. Why had Wrangler invented the button fly? One button was bad enough, unfastening four while trying to maintain tongue-lock was nearly impossible. After several failed attempts, Ryan pulled back and laughed, then reached down and flicked the damned things free like it was nothing.

"You should see me do that with my teeth." He smirked.

I'd seen his cock before, but here, in the light of my bedroom, it was a wonder to behold. He noticed my widened eyes and laughed again as he stood on the bed, craning his neck to avoid the ceiling fan, then peeled off his jeans.

As God intended, he wasn't wearing underwear. Let the angels sing.

"You're so going to hell for that," the little angel's voice whispered in my head.

"Not a chance. Look at that thing. Angels should *sing about it,"* the devil rebutted.

"You really have to stop being amazed. I mean, I get it. It's glorious." He did his best Vanna White hand wave at his very large letter D. "It's all yours. No need to be intimidated."

I grunted a laugh, leaned forward, and took his cock in my mouth all the way to his balls.

Yeah, I overreached.

The gag that ensued sent Ryan into a fit of laughter that totally blew any sexy mood we had going on. For the first time that day, his tears were borne of happiness. The fucker took that moment to reach down and tickle my ribs—which are, like the rest of me, highly sensitive. I curled into the fetal position and howled like a newborn being slapped on

the rump that first time. Ryan took that as encouragement, sat his weight on my legs to hold me down, and
intensified his attack.

Right there, in the middle of my own goddamned
bed, with the man of my dreams naked and erect, I
peed all over everything. Not the demure little dribble
one might mistake for sweat or something, a geyser of
gold to rival the tallest of McDonald's golden arches.

If I live to be a hundred, I will never turn that deep
crimson again. It's not possible.

Ryan practically fell off the bed, he was laughing
so hard.

I leapt up, retrieved a towel from the bathroom,
and stripped the bedding. Ryan helped, though I
avoided making eye contact as he cackled throughout
our first domestic activity. Once the sheets and
comforter were on the floor and the mattress pad was
wiped down, I looked up.

"That's my only set. I'll need to go to the laundry
room before we can sleep in this bed."

We were both still naked. In the embarrassment of
the moment, I'd forgotten that. Ryan hadn't.

He stepped forward and shoved my chest with
both hands. We tumbled together back onto the bed.

"There's no way you're putting clothes back on.
We have unfinished business."

His hand found my now-flaccid penis and went to

work. His mouth did the same, and we were soon locked in a tongue dance for the ages.

"Where's your lube?"

I pointed to the side table drawer. When he leaned across me, stretching to his full length, I took him in my mouth again. The sound of a drawer opening was drowned out by the snap and pop of vigorous sucking and slurping. The salt of his sweat was nothing compared to the tang of his pre-cum. I ran my tongue over his opening and licked him clean. When his body quivered, I redoubled my efforts, gripping his balls in one hand, while cupping the base of his shaft with the other and sucking him vigorously.

He grunted, dropped the lube, and rolled onto his back so I had a better angle. Over the next several minutes, he pulled my head up, urging me to stop lest he finish before we ever got started. I ignored him and dove back down, desperate to give him half the pleasure his kisses had given me. A dribble of pre-cum became pulses of tang as he filled my throat.

Still, I didn't stop.

His back was now arched, his chest taut, his abs clenched in chiseled splendor. I ran my hand over them, feeling every crease, the hardness of his muscles. I thought he would soften, having fed me his load, but his cock only stiffened further. I looked up, dick in mouth, to find him staring down the length of his shaking body. I let him fall from my mouth but kept my hand gripping his base. He was so fucking perfect.

I swallowed the last of his contribution as I reached down for the fallen bottle. The pump had cracked. When I raised it from the floor, slippery liquid spilled across Ryan's chest and stomach.

"Shit, that's cold." He started to sit up. I pushed him back down and set the bottle on the night stand.

"You, stay still." He quirked a grin, enjoying the evil glint in my eye as I took both hands and smeared the lube across his pecs, over one arm then the other, then his abs. Finally, when he shone like a Roman statue in the rain, I slicked his cock. He threw his head back and moaned as I rubbed his head with one palm while my other hand stroked the length of his shaft. Despite his orgasm, he was still fully aroused.

I took one hand and moistened my hole, slipping a finger in to ready myself. Then, with his head still back and eyes closed, I lifted myself and guided him inside me. His hands reached up to grip my hips, but I grabbed them and leaned over his body to hold them above his head. Our lips were inches apart. I could taste his breath. I pressed my butt down and drove him deeper inside me as our bodies pressed together, smooth with oily wetness. There was no friction, but there was definitely heat.

Fire.

Holding his hands in place, I ground him in and out. His kisses became a torrent of hunger, of need, of desire.

I released his hands, and he wrapped his arms around me, pulling him into me. His cock found my prostate and I cried out, arching my back. Driven by my pleasure, Ryan's strong arms flipped me onto my back, careful to keep his pulsating cock deep inside me. Oil dripped from his chest as he rose above me. His hands squeezed my shoulder, then my chest, coating my body like I'd done his. He grabbed my dick, but I pushed his hands away, unwilling to let this end.

"Fuck me harder, faster," I begged.

He grunted and slammed himself forward. Our skin slapped, his balls ground against my butt. The bed squealed in protest. Every thrust sent an echo of something—something primal—screaming through my body.

He pumped faster, and his moans grew louder. Then he stopped, and I felt his hands grip my shoulders. Again, without removing himself, he flipped me over and spooned me from behind. I hadn't thought he could go any deeper, but now learned how wrong I had been. I tried to relax, but the thrill he sent through me caused my whole body to tense. He hardened more each time I clenched.

"Oh, God. I'm so close," he said through gritted teeth.

"Don't stop. Please."

He didn't.

With one last maneuver, he pressed me face down and spread my legs, arching my butt toward him again. I gripped the corners of the bed, my arms stretched as wide as my legs. Every muscle in my oil-slicked arms and stomach flexed, and my ass clutched his dick like a vise. I felt his pulse quicken through the throbbing of his cock. I couldn't believe he lived in my body. My mind raced. My heart danced. My body shook.

His thrusts were now so fast I could barely take a breath between them. He grunted with every push, loud and deep, somewhere between growl and groan. His sweat dripped hotter than the lube. He interlaced our fingers as he bent over me, thrusting, until he released one last cry in time with his body's explosion.

I could feel the heat of his life within. It was his second time, yet thrust after thrust sent more of him inside me. I reveled in the thought of us becoming one.

He started to pull away, but I reached back and held him. "Don't pull out."

"It's your turn."

"I want you inside me when I cum."

He bit my ear, and my butt squeezed. "Ahhh," he called out.

"That's what you get for biting. Now do your job, mister."

He grunted, then reached around and began stroking me. I'll never know how he stayed hard, but as he rubbed my dick, his own began thrusting once more. I didn't last long. Every part of my body cried out for release. Ryan's hand obliged.

Sticky, sweaty, and slick, we lay spooning, Ryan inside me.

Neither of us dared move.

We fell asleep as one.

27

HOME SWEET HOME

I woke the next morning to the warmth of Ryan's body pressed against mine. One arm still held me close. I could hear his slow, steady breathing as he slept. We'd fallen asleep with him inside me—the thought of which made me giddy—but sometime in the night, he'd popped out. I guessed even his eternal erection had to subside at some point. Little Michael was jealous of his staying power.

After a delicate un-sticking, I watched Ryan for a few moments. His normally perfect hair was thoroughly mussed. I reached down and moved it out of his face, and there were those lips—one normal, the other slightly puffy. It reminded me of a model who'd gone to the wrong plastic surgeon. How had I seen it as a flaw, a reason to strike him from the list? Staring down at his sleeping form, I couldn't imagine a more perfect feature on a man. I loved how that lip felt as it pressed tenderly against mine, how it tasted when I swirled it with my tongue or nibbled it with my teeth.

It was part of Ryan, and I loved it.

He didn't stir, so I rose and walked into the kitchen to make coffee. The air conditioner had been on full blast and, without clothing or Ryan's arms to keep me warm, I regretted not throwing on a T-shirt and shorts. The coffee maker took several minutes to heat water, so I did what everyone did when boiling water—I leaned back and watched it intently.

"You know that doesn't make it heat quicker."

I nearly jumped out of my shorts—well, I would've if I'd had any on.

Ryan wrapped his arms around me and, despite his chuckle at my jumpiness, I leaned into him.

"Good morning." He kissed my neck.

I turned to face him, wrapping my arms around his back. "Good morning to you too."

"So, it's Sunday. Pretty good day to look at houses."

I pulled back.

He raised his palms. "I need a place to live, and you volunteered to help me find one, remember?"

"Right, sorry. Guess I need this coffee more than I thought." I let out the breath I'd been holding.

I poured each of us a mug, then added three

hazelnut creamers and one Splenda. We liked our coffee the same way. Try not to gag at the sweetness of that.

Thirty minutes later, we'd both showered and thrown on clothes—something I was disappointed to see as he walked back into the den in faded khaki shorts and a green Journey T-shirt.

"Journey?" I pointed at his chest.

"Yeah, my all-time favorite band."

"No freakin' way. They're my all-time."

Yes, another saccharine-soaked moment. Get used to it.

We scanned the newspaper for townhouse listings, then logged into AOL and pulled up a couple realtor sites. Once we had a list of ten potential townhouses, we set our mugs in the sink and headed out.

There was a comfortable normalcy in that morning. We weren't doing anything earth-shattering—just waking, having coffee, and driving around town—but it felt right. I remember staring out the window of his car as we drove past the first few possibilities. He ruled them out from the street—but the simple act of us discussing their pros and cons struck me. He wanted my opinion. He cared what I thought, what I liked and disliked about each home.

We really were doing this together.

And it was the most natural thing in the world.

If my twenty-two-year-old self could see me then, he would've scoffed at the idea of two dudes holding hands as they drove around town, looking at houses and talking about landscaping. He would've ridiculed the sinful nature of their union. He would've been sickened.

That guy really was an ignorant asshole. I might've made a million mistakes since then, but I'd learned to love more than hate, to respect rather than scorn. I'd come a long way in only a few years. A spark of pride bloomed at that thought.

Now there was a *we* in the conversation.

<hr>

THE BED WAS NEATLY MADE WITH FRESHLY CLEANED sheets by the time Ryan got back to my apartment the next day. He'd spent much of his afternoon at his company's local office, going over pitches submitted by travel agencies vying for their business. I was in the kitchen cutting carrots and onions when the key rattled in the lock.

God, that was a beautiful sound.

"I'm home."

Home. He'd called my apartment *home;* he called *being with me* home.

Every ounce of sappiness in me welled up and I

had to fight back the tears. The last thing I needed was to let this incredible man think I was a perpetual puddle of mush.

"It feels so good to call this place home and see you first thing when I'm done with my day." He'd out-mushed me.

A tear slipped free. I tried to recover. "Darn onions."

"Come here. Let me get that." He spread his arms wide. I raced around the counter and fell into them, nuzzling my nose into the space between his neck and collarbone. I'd found that spot last night during one of our flips and knew instantly it would be my favorite place in the world. I sucked in a long breath, drawing in as much of his scent as I could hold. He held me close and kissed the top of my head.

"I missed you today," he whispered.

When I pulled my face out of his neck, tears were flowing freely. He reached up and wiped them.

"What's all this?" he asked.

I beamed through my leakage. "This doesn't feel real yet. It's everything I want, but feels a little over-whelming. I don't think I've ever been this happy."

His lips held mine for a long moment, then he drew back.

"I found another townhouse we need to look at."

That wasn't what I expected—not that I had any

particular conversation in mind in that blissful moment.

"Oh, where?"

"Roswell. It's a two-unit building. From what I can see in the ad, all the houses around it are single-family. The best part; it's on a cul-de-sac, so the street's quiet and there are only a handful of neighbors. It's two streets off the main strip, so we'd be close to everything."

There was that *we* again.

We were looking for a home for *him*. When had this become something else? Was I reading too much into his words, hearing what my heart hoped to hear? I did that sometimes. It's a Pisces thing. We daydream and sometimes blur the line between reality and what we wish reality would be. I rather liked living in my daydreams, but they could impede clear-thinking at times.

"I want you to move in with me when I get my new place."

I stumbled back a pace. "You want…what? Really?" Did he seriously just ask me to move in with him? "What about Diane and the kids? What will she think? We've only known each other a few months. Is this smart? Are we rushing things? Dwayne would kill me. Connie…she adores you. Never mind her. Are you serious?"

He chuckled at the torrent of questions. "Yes, I'm serious. Diane will be fine—in time. I'll continue seeing the kids at her place. She'd prefer that, even if I lived alone. You'll have to be patient with everything. It's going to get rough before it gets better, and I'll probably be hard to handle some days. Are you okay with that?"

My smile became a serious line. After a moment's thought, I nodded. "I'll support you, no matter what. I can't imagine what she's going through, what the kids will go through—and you'll need to be there for them —but you are *my* priority, and I'll be there when *you* need me."

His brow furrowed, then his mouth set as he cupped my cheek. "Michael, listen to me. Yes, we're still new—and yes, this *is* crazy—but I know what I want. I want *you* to be the last thing I see before I fall asleep, and the first thing I see when I wake up. Every day."

I don't remember if I spoke. The next thing I knew, he'd stepped forward and held my head firmly in both hands, forcing my eyes to his. It would be the first time I ever saw his lip quiver as he spoke.

"I love you, Michael, more than anything. We'll face it all together." His thumbs stroked my cheeks. "Will you live with me?"

My voice was a pitiful squeal, but I managed a

"yes" before the cutest lip in the world pressed passionately into mine.

That was the moment I released all control and surrendered the last of my self-protective walls. That was the moment I gave myself fully to Ryan.

Carrots and onions forgotten, we found ourselves naked and filling each other with love—and everything else.

Fuck, there went the sheets again. We'd be spending another night naked without bedcoverings.

I really needed to buy another set.

28

STRAWBERRIES AND CHAMPAGNE

Three weeks later, Ryan made an offer on the townhouse in Roswell. We closed two weeks after that.

Our new home was exactly as he'd described it: half of a large, two-story house on a secluded cul-de-sac with ten other single-family houses. Yards were neatly tended, but not pretentiously so. Massive oak and pine trees towered over everything, casting dancing shadows on the street. Most of the houses were several decades old, and there was little uniformity to their construction, giving the neighborhood an eclectic, cozy feel. The front porch of the neighbor immediately across the street was littered with colorful plants and ceramic statues of animals and gnomes. A rainbow flag fluttered on a pole above the front door. The lesbians-in-residence, a couple who'd been together for more than thirty years, were the first on the street to welcome us.

Ryan rented a truck and retrieved what few things he was taking from his marriage. He felt strongly about his role in supporting his family. As he put it, he was the cause of their marriage ending, so he should support them, no matter what. Diane offered to sell the house and split the proceeds. He refused, insisting she stay, and offered to sign the deed into her name. He argued that the kids needed stability, and that was *their* home. It was hers too. With the exception of a bedroom suite they'd used in a guest room, a recliner, and a coffee table from their game room, he relinquished all the furnishings as well.

In the end, he volunteered to pay more in child support than was ordered, and agreed to alimony above what the law required. He was determined Diane and the kids would not suffer beyond the emotional toll that was unavoidable.

He never wavered in putting them ahead of himself, and my respect for him grew with each decision.

Despite the two-month notice period with my apartment, we moved my things into the townhouse the week after closing and quickly fell into a comfortable routine. Ryan joined my gym so we could work out each night together. Aside from getting to spend more time together, he was a fantastic training partner, never giving me more than a moment's rest, no matter how much I grumbled. I cooked most nights. There was something in the simple act of making dinner for us that gave me satisfaction I hadn't known before. It felt like I was doing something special for him with each meal—and that man could eat.

Even the act of going to bed became a ritual I found endearing. By the time we finished our work-out, then finished dinner and cleaned the kitchen, it was dark outside and we were both exhausted. We would read in bed before shutting off the lights, Ryan some business or self-help book, me an epic fantasy.

Ryan loved to be touching, almost as much as I craved it. He would hold me as we drifted to sleep. But even in the middle of the night, when one of us would roll away from the embrace, our hands would touch, or his foot would find mine and remain in contact until we woke. I barely remember a night when I woke without some part of us connected. I had never felt so loved; had never loved so deeply.

OUR NEIGHBORHOOD TOOK THEIR HOLIDAYS seriously. When Santa was a month from his big ride, colorful lights, shimmering angels, fanciful reindeer, and enough tinsel to bury Tinsel Town in silver splashed across the lawns surrounding us. Our tiny patch of grass, which was more brown than green since fall had surrendered to winter, was a pitiful reminder that we needed to get into the holiday spirit —and fast.

We spent one Saturday tree shopping, stopping at Caribou for some pumpkin-flavored foo-foo drink Ryan swore would change my life. I'll admit, it was tasty, but there was nothing life changing in that cup, no matter what he said.

We decided to go the tasteful route, one that would meet with Ryan's mother's approval. Strings of steady clear-white lights outlined our roof, while netting with matching lights stretched over the hedgerow. A lone holly bush rose from the ground about twenty yards in front of our house. Ryan couldn't resist shaping it like a Christmas tree and putting a blinky star topper on its tip. It was *sort of* classy—probably over the line for his prudish mom—which meant I loved it.

When the actual holiday week rolled around, we celebrated apart. It was Ryan's holiday with his kids, so they drove north to spent time with his parents. I drove back to Nashville to celebrate Santa with the pack. Both trips proved uneventful—unless you counted us ducking away from our families to talk on the phone several times a day. We were young and romantic as hell. I'd say we were hopelessly romantic, but we were actually quite hope*ful*.

Life returned to its relaxed routine once Santa found his way back to the North Pole. Basketball was again in a mid-season frenzy, and I officiated five or six nights each week. That stole from our time together, but made the moments we shared that much sweeter. Funny how it works that way, isn't it?

DID SOMEONE ORDER LIMES?

I was born on my mother's birthday, the twelfth of March.

That meant two things.

First, it wasn't just a celebration of my birth, it was "our day," as my mom called it. Before the whole *gay thing* happened—yes, that's what she called *that*—we were close. Our day would spark personal celebrations, usually involving the two of us escaping the rest of the pack to spend the day doing whatever we fancied in the moment. I've often missed that closeness with her.

Second, according to astrologers, when one is born on his mother's birthday, all the attributes ascribed to his birth sign—and the rising and falling moons and suns and whatever else they say counts—are doubled. Double is my interpretation. The astrology books I half-mockingly read used terms like "exponential increase" or "multiplication factor." I've never fully believed in all that, but I can tell you one thing. Every description of a Pisces I've ever read fits me perfectly, and the whole psycho Pisces addendum due to *our day* also makes some weird cosmic sense. We both share a creepy intuition, as well as an empathic sense that would make Miss Dione jealous. More importantly for our conversation, it made me feel *everything* deeply, especially emotions related to sentiment.

Let's face it. I was a mush pit.

Stop snickering. It's endearing. Right?

When my birthday rolled around, the psycho Pisces in me anticipated grand gestures of rose petals and incense, gifts wrapped in silk, and champagne bubbling out of gold-rimmed flutes. When Ryan left for work without so much as a birthday kiss, I was disappointed. When lunch rolled around, and he didn't come home to surprise me with naked goodness—or at least a cheesecake—I was disheartened.

By two o'clock, I hadn't received a single birthday phone call or email.

Not from Connie.

Not even from Dwayne.

I called Dwayne. He *never* forgot.

His phone rang until the machine picked up.

Yes, kids, it was an actual machine, not the built-in voice thingy we have these days.

Anyway, I left a quick message, not mentioning that it was my birthday. Every Pisces will understand this: it was *their* job to remember, not my job to remind, otherwise, it wouldn't mean anything.

Can I get a Piscean amen? Anyone?

I needed a pick-me-up—badly. So I dialed the one person who *always* made me smile: Connie.

"Hey, sweet pea."

"Hey, Con."

"Oh, honey. Why do you sound down? What did Ryan do now?"

I chuckled. I loved that mama bear.

"He's wonderful, hasn't done anything. Guess I'm just a little blue."

"Isn't it your birthday? You're not allowed to be blue on your birthday. It's the law."

I was grinning already. She remembered. "Yeah, I know. Guess some people are just rebels."

"Well, happy birthday." There was commotion in the background, probably Think!ers making a muck of something. "Hey, I need to run. Ted's at it again. Don't you miss this place?"

I laughed. "Not even a little. I miss you tons, though."

"Aww. Miss you too. Let's spend Saturday together. Do a tour of barriers in town or something."

I chuckled at our old joke, but couldn't hide my disappointment with her inability to spend time with me on *my* day.

"Sounds great. Looking forward to it."

I hung up. Woe-is-me wasn't my normal color, but I was wearing it with pride that day.

Then, for a brief moment, there was a glimmer of hope. Ryan called from work around four o'clock and told me to dress for dinner. He'd made a reservation at some swanky place I'd never heard of. It sounded expensive. My heart danced a little jig.

"This'll be beautiful, just us, babe. I want to make you feel special."

By the time I hung up, my heart was full, warm, and fuzzy—and that's a hard combination to hold in one's chest at the same time.

Two and a half hours later, we drove into the lot of the Hilton. Nikolai's Roof was the legendary restaurant on the hotel's thirtieth floor, offering breathtaking views of the city and a mouthwatering menu that featured house-infused vodkas, caviar, and a dessert menu to make the czar's toes curl. I'd heard about the place a thousand times, but never dreamed of eating there.

Ryan wore black slacks with a crisp white button-down. I settled on my best jeans, a forest green long-sleeve shirt, and a black leather jacket. As the elevator doors opened and we got our first peek, Ryan leaned over and said, "I think we're a tad underdressed."

I thought we looked like a million bucks. Screw all those stuffy folks in their ties and dresses.

He nibbled the top of my ear, and all thoughts of clothing evaporated.

"May I help you, sir?" the maître d' asked, his thick Slavic accent purring with each word.

Ryan stepped forward. "Yes, thank you. Reservation for Lowell. I believe Lina has the room prepared."

The maître d' scanned his book, then looked up meaningfully at Ryan. "Of course, Mr. Lowell. Follow me, please."

We followed the man who was dressed—and waddled—like a penguin.

I elbowed Ryan and leaned in to whisper, "Did you slip him a twenty? What was with that look he gave you?"

Ryan shrugged.

My Pisces Spidey sense stirred. *Shit*. He was up to something.

We walked all the way around the circular floor, past dozens of tables. The food was as elegant as the guests. Every server we passed smiled in greeting and bowed at the waist. Their gestures of respect, along with their deep maroon waistcoats with tails, made the whole affair feel like traversing the court of Czar Nicholas—before that pesky revolution took it all away from him.

As we made the final turn in our circle, the maître d' turned sharply to his left and waddled into the center of the column. A stylized door covered in gilding and deeply carved Russian lettering barred our way. Our guide rapped one white-gloved knuckle against the door, then turned the knob to allow us entry.

The first thing I saw was a wall of flowers. On the far wall hung hundreds of glass vials, with a fresh flower protruding from each. The effect of hundreds of flowers of every variety and color splashed across a black wall and lit by strategically placed spotlights was stunning. Equally beautiful flowers overflowed from ornate vases displayed at precise intervals on the table. Even the buffet against the near wall was etched with gold and laden with flora.

This was a private dining room, designed for no more than twelve, but the room *felt* massive.

Ryan's hand on the small of my back guided me forward toward the table. I was so distracted by the ambiance that I'd yet to look at the table—specifically, at how many places were set. In a world-class restaurant with an eye for detail such as this, nothing was done without purpose. Why was the table set for four? And why were two of the chairs already filled?

My eyes raised from the tablecloth and caught on a crystal tumbler filled to the brim with limes.

Something felt *so* familiar about that.

I looked up. My head cocked to one side, trying to process what my eyes were seeing. I was baffled.

"Dwayne?"

My gayfather, the greatest friend and sherpa to ever wear the rainbow robe, smiled up at me.

I still didn't get it.

"Connie?"

She was sitting next to Dwayne.

She giggled and waved.

I turned to Ryan. He was beaming.

"We're here for your birthday, dummy. Ryan flew me down," Dwayne said.

My breath caught as a hand flew to cover my gaping mouth. I knew what was happening, but I couldn't believe it. At thirty years old, no one had *ever* thrown a birthday party for me. The pack never had much money, so there was little joy there. I was a band nerd in high school, so popular kids coming over to wish me well wasn't in the cards either.

Ryan had arranged my first birthday party.

He'd kept it secret, coordinated with the people I

loved most, even flew one of them hundreds of miles just for dinner. I knew how amazing this was, but my brain struggled to accept its reality.

"What do you think?" Ryan asked, his husky whisper tickling my ear.

"I…Ryan…that's Dwayne…and Connie. Why—?"

He laughed, one of those deep-in-the-belly rumbles that made a whole room feel merry and bright. Connie and Dwayne joined him, adding a tenor and soprano to his baritone.

It was the most beautiful melody I'd ever heard.

I looked from Connie to Dwayne, then to Ryan, each of whom was smiling broadly. One of the servers pulled my chair back and motioned for me to claim the table's head as Ryan walked around and sat in the seat opposite.

We dined on the finest filet, sampled exquisite vodkas, savored the deepest, most aromatic wines— and laughed like there was no tomorrow. Connie's perky, sometimes snarky jibes, mixed with Dwayne's dry attempts at humor, had Ryan and me practically peeing our pants at the table. At one point, I noticed two of the ever-present servers hiding chuckles of their own. The evening was as delightful as it was delicious—and Ryan had done it all for me.

That just blew my mind.

For me.

Midway through dessert—the *fourth* course of the evening—I had one of those *Matrix* moments. The room froze. Everyone's motion stilled. Even the sounds of the diners outside halted. I was the only one able to move and see and feel. Connie was frozen mid-giggle, Dwayne had his drink halfway to his mouth, and Ryan was—Ryan was staring at me. His gaze was intense, his eyes curled upward. His mouth was set, not in a frown, but a pose of deep considera-tion. There was such depth to his gaze, such warmth—and *love*. I could've stared into that gaze for a lifetime.

Unfortunately, the maître d' found the pause button, and everyone started moving again. Connie coughed and held a linen napkin to her mouth as her giggle died. Dwayne downed the last of his Jack and Coke. The servers finished clearing our dessert plates. And Ryan—

Ryan's gaze remained.

His gaze at me.

Right there, across a table in one of the fanciest restaurants around, I saw the depth of his love. I saw it in his eyes, in the set of his jaw. I saw it in the thoughtful tending to *every* detail the evening offered.

I'd always said I'd know when the right man came along because everyone in the room would disappear when our eyes met. I would forget anyone else existed. He would consume my attention, my desire, my need.

In that moment, lost in pools of steely gray, everyone around us faded into the background. The scurrying servers vanished. Connie and Dwayne became blurs in the periphery. But Ryan—my beautiful, strong, amazing Ryan—he sharpened into focus. His poochy lip quirked into a lopsided smile, and my heart soared.

A life flashed before my eyes. Not a life lived and passing, but one yet to come. I saw lunches and dinner parties, vacations and quiet evenings, adventures and trials. Woven throughout every chapter, every scene played out on the stage of my mind's eye, was the man sitting before me. I let my inner Pisces take control and dream with unfettered abandon.

And Ryan's gaze remained.

EPILOGUE

My Dearest Reader,

Thank you for sticking with me through our latest adventure. This period of my life wove together beautiful moments, challenges, and lessons for which I am thankful.

I've been overwhelmed by your feedback to this series. I've received emails about scenes taking readers back to their youth, to happy first loves, and even to the grief that comes with loss. Each message is special and very much appreciated.

Some feedback repeated itself enough that I feel the need to respond en masse. Two examples:

1. Comments regarding crazy situations that might seem impausible were not lost to the ether.

2. Others who expressed justified concerns over the lack of condoms and safe sex were also heard.

At the end of the next—and final—book in this series, I will answer questions and respond to concerns raised throughout.

No, this isn't typical, especially in a romance series, but nothing about this series has been typical. Why start now?

Thank you for understanding and enjoying the ride.

And yes, I said *ride*. Stop it, you naughty sausage.

Casey

Get your copy of My Last Date to continue Michael's (my) journey.

BEFORE YOU GO

If you enjoyed My Wildest Date, please take a moment to leave a review filled with stars. Your feedback helps indie authors thrive and grow, giving you more steam and romance to enjoy for years to come.

LET'S STAY IN TOUCH!

Keep up to date through my newsletter, or check me out on Facebook or Instagram. I love interacting with readers and incorporating your ideas into future stories.

www.ingramcontent.com/pod-product-compliance
Lightning Source LLC
Chambersburg PA
CBHW070447300726

48975CB00007B/2069